Billy You, No More Hills

Clarence W. Leslie

Copyright © 2015 Clarence W. Leslie
All rights reserved
First Edition

PAGE PUBLISHING, INC.
New York, NY

First originally published by Page Publishing, Inc. 2015

ISBN 978-1-68213-885-4 (pbk)
ISBN 978-1-68213-886-1 (digital)

Printed in the United States of America

Chapter 1

Dropping down on one knee, Billy reached under the canvas cot he used as a bed. He pulled out a small grip, the kind that each boy used to store his clothes in. The small grip was all that was needed. Each boy had two sets of clothes, the one he had on and the one called his change, which was kept folded up neatly in the grip.

Billy's cot was set down at the end of a hall next to a door that said Fire Exit. He wasn't blocking the door, so it was legal for him to sleep there. But Billy hadn't always slept in the hall.

A little over two years ago, there had been four more boys than beds in the home, so Mrs. Jamison, head matron, had placed some fold-up canvas cots in the hall to make bed space for all "her boys," as she liked to call them. At the time, Billy had his own bunk bed in the room for the eight to twelve-year-olds.

Mrs. Jamison moved Billy into the hall along with three other boys, giving his bunk to a new kid. Billy was upset, but no way was he going to let it show! He didn't want the head matron to have the satisfaction of knowing that it bothered him.

Billy was nine years old at the time; he had been in the home all his life, except for a short period when he had been placed in a foster home. He had been in the foster home for just three weeks when, without any explanation, he was brought back. Mrs. Jamison seemed unhappy about his return, but Billy didn't care how she felt. He was glad to be back.

And now, Billy, twelve years old, was getting ready to go to another foster home. He rolled up the pad he used as a mattress, then folded up the cot.

Billy was the only boy still sleeping in the hall—the other boys had stayed there only a month. He could have gone back to the bunk room also; instead, he asked Mrs. Jamison if he could stay where he was. She had readily agreed, and to Billy, it seemed as if she was pleased that he had wanted to stay in the hall.

There were two doors in the hallway, both on the same side of the hall. Billy opened the first door. Working his way through the piled-up furniture in the room, he hid his cot and mattress, hoping no one would find them and take over his spot at the end of the hall.

Then Billy opened the second door and entered a room lined with shelves jammed full of books—schoolbooks. Billy supposed that like the furniture in the other room, the books had all been donated to the home. Billy had sure made full use of these books!

All the boys in the Orphans' Home—there were no girls—went to school for four hours a day, every day of the year except weekend and holidays. After lunch period, the boys had two hours of assigned chores, then one hour of study period back in the school room. No books were ever allowed to leave the school room. If you didn't get your study assignment finished in that one hour, the next day you sat for two hours studying while the rest of the boys were outside on recreation time.

And recreation time was the part of the day the boys all liked the best—this was the time they were turned loose with very little supervision. They could run and play all they pleased as long as there was no trouble or fighting.

But it was the books—the books in the storage room—that Billy used to full advantage. At straight up 9:00 p.m., all the boys had to be in bed and all the lights out. At ten minutes to nine, one of the lady assistants would walk through the recreation room and bunk rooms, telling everyone "Lights out" in ten minutes, and that in exactly ten minutes, the rooms would go dark.

Except the light hanging down from a cord in the ceiling over Billy's bed and the lights in the kitchen, which was right down the hall from where Billy slept. But at the same time, the other lights went out. Billy pulled the cord hanging from his light, turning it off. He would lie in his cot, listening to the boys on the opposite side of the wall, settling down on to their bunks with a few quiet good-nights to each other, as there was no talking allowed after lights out. After all movement had ceased and all was quiet, Billy would quietly slip out of bed, go to the room full of books, and pick out a book that he wanted to study that night. He loved history, but he liked all the schoolbooks, English, spelling, math, and any book that pertained to school.

After he got the book that he wanted for that certain night, he would turn his light back on and lie there and study for two hours or more. He did this most nights. He wasn't really studying as much as he was learning. Of course he knew that even if he wasn't studying at night, he would still be the smartest kid in school. He liked to rub it in, but he didn't like to think of himself as being a smart aleck or cocky, but inside he knew that he was.

In class, the teacher would tell the pupils to open their books to chapter so-and-so on page so-and-so and study for the upcoming test. The other students would open their book to the right page and dig in to studying hard.

Billy's desk was on the outside row of desks where he could look out the window. Sometimes when the teacher gave them a subject to study, Billy deliberately would not open his book, setting with his hands folded on his desk while staring out the window. He knew that this would annoy the teacher. He didn't do it every day, but most of them, and on those days, the teacher would quietly get up so as not to disturb the other students and walk down the row of desks and either take hold of his ear giving it a twist or give him a sharp rap on his folded hands with her blackboard pointer, then she would bend over and whisper sharply in his ear, "*Study*." She never really hurt him when she pulled his ear or rapped him on the knuckles; it was just a friendly reminder. Needless to say, when the test papers were turned in, he always got an A. This puzzled the teacher and upset the rest of the boys in his class. It put a smug smile of satisfaction on his face as he strolled down the aisle to his desk holding the test paper so all the kids in the class could see it.

Billy, with the grip in his hand, walked down to the kitchens. He was ready to go meet his new foster parents. He wasn't ready to go because he wanted to; he was ready to go because they wanted him to. He glanced heavenward and said, Thanks for all the help you didn't give me again, it seems like every time I ask you for a little something, you're always helping someone else, or maybe you're just sitting up there in an easy chair looking down on me and laughing. Billy had this ongoing argument with God, it wasn't a bad argument. It was kind of like he was using God for someone to complain to, as he didn't have anyone else to tell his troubles to or blame his troubles on. He didn't get far out of line with God, but he sure as heck didn't back down from him. Billy figured if he did something wrong and got in hot water over it that was his doing.

But something like what happening to him today wasn't his fault, and it had to be blamed on someone. He looked up and said, "That someone is you."

In the kitchen, Mr. Cook was getting his pots and pans out, preparing to fix lunch for the kids. All the boys thought it was funny that a cook was named Mr. Cook. But he had straightened that situation out real fast. Mr. Cook had been at the home just a little over three years now. On the first day there he had walked out of the kitchen into the mess hall, when he had reached the far in end of the room, he turned and placing his hands on his hips he said, "I am your new cook, and my name is Mr. Cook." Some of the kids began to giggle but stopped real fast when Mr. Cook shot a mean glance down their way. "Now let me tell you something about myself. Before I came here, I cooked on a merchant ship. I have been in every port in the world." He paused a moment, looking the kids over. "I've cooked for a lot of men in my day, some good, some bad, and some men that were downright mean. But no matter how bad or how mean they were, they called me Mr. Cook, and they did not laugh, because I will not stand for that, and I will not stand being called Cookie. Now if you think that you might want to call me Cookie, before you do, you had better to look up some of those mean, bad ones I was telling you about and ask them what happened when they called me Cookie. Now that is all I've got to say, except I never want to hear any one of you complaining about my cooking. If you think calling me Cookie makes me mad, that is nothing compared to what will happen to you for bad-mouthing the food that I put on the mess tables for you. Now does everyone in this room understand what I'm telling you? There was dead silence; no one moved, and no one seemed to be breathing. He stood there a long moment staring at them all, then in a thundering voice, he shouted, "Well?"

In unison, they shouted back, "Yes, sir." Some of them even jumped up and stood at attention. Without another word, he stomped down between mess tables and on into the kitchen. That was the quietest meal eaten there that anyone could remember, and as far as anyone knew, Mr. Cook was never called Cookie and for as the food that he put on the tables, there was no reason to complain; they were the best prepared meals that the boys had ever eaten.

Now as Billy entered the kitchen, Mr. Cook looked his way and at the grip in his hand. "You leaving us, boy?"

"Yes, sir," Billy said.

Turning back to a big pile of bread dough he was kneading, he said, "Take care of yourself, boy."

"Thank you, sir."

To Mr. Cook, all the kids in the home were Boy. From the kitchen, Billy went through the mess hall to the bunk rooms on the left; this is where the smaller boys, aged four to eight, slept. On the opposite side of the mess hall was where the nine- to seventeen-year-olds' bunk beds were.

As each boy turned eighteen, they had to leave the home. It wasn't as bad as it sounded; they had a job waiting for them through the home, which had connections with the merchants in towns nearby, and they were given enough money to survive on until they received their first paycheck. Billy couldn't wait until it was his turn.

All the kids knew Billy was leaving; there were three or four of them about his age or a little older that were glad to see him go. But not the smaller boys. He was their favorite. He was their champion. He was the one that stopped the bigger boys from taking the desserts away from the little ones at meal time. He was the one that stopped the big boys from picking on the little ones.

And as he walked into the room, he could see it in their eyes. All eleven of them standing in a group. Their champion was leaving. He glanced up. "It's not just me you're hurting. Look at these little guys, they need me, but what do you care?" As he went to the huddled group, he tilted his head up again. "Heck, as far as I know, you might not be listening. Well, don't you worry about me. Mr. Cook told me to take care of myself, and that's what I'm going to do. But I'm putting these little ones in your care. How does it feel to get a bit of responsibility shoved right back at you?" Of these boys, little Arty was the one he thought the most of. There were tears in Arty's eyes as Billy kneeled down and put his arms around him. "Hey, what's wrong? I've never seen my buddy crying before."

Trying to hold back his sobs Arty answered, "You're leaving, and now I'm going to be here all by myself."

"Hey, what are you talking about? Look at all your friends here, and there's Mr. Cook and all the other people around you."

Arty said, "They don't count if you're not here."

Billy patted him on the back, saying, "I won't be gone long. If anyone picks on you or is mean to you, just let me know when I get back, and I'll punch their lights out. OK?"

At that moment, Mrs. Jameson stepped into the doorway, saying, "Billy, your people are waiting, come on."

Billy wanted to say, "They are not my people," but he didn't want to make her angry on his last day there. He gave Arty another hug and told the other boys good-bye and that he hoped to be seeing them soon.

Taking his grip, he went out and down the hall to the waiting room, where parents came to pick the kid they were adopting and where his people were waiting to take him to another foster home. Probably to do all their chores and yard work around their house. Like the other foster families did. The moment he saw them, he was sure that he knew them. But that was impossible; the only folks he knew were right here in the home. They were both tall and gaunt looking. The lady had graying hair pulled straight back against her head and tied in a bun at the back and wore a plain brown-colored dress. The man had on blue work pants and a blue work shirt. His hair was thin and combed straight back. He had on some old-fashioned eyeglasses.

Mrs. Jamison came over, put her hand on his shoulder, and said, "Billy, this is Mr. and Mrs. Rob Adams, and you will be going to stay with them for a while. Now they are going to treat you just like a son, and you are going to accept them as your parents. Do you understand?"

To himself, he said, *No, ma'am, I don't understand.* Rolling his eyes up, he said, *Do you?*

But to Mrs. Jamison, he answered, "Yes, ma'am, I understand."

She patted him on the shoulder again. "Good, you be a good boy and don't cause these nice folks any problems." With that, she turned around and walked away.

Mr. and Mrs. Adams turned and walked the other way toward the big front door, going outside. Mrs. Adams tagged along behind Mr. Adams, and Billy tagged along behind her. Outside the door, there was a small porch with five steps leading down to the walkway. At the bottom of the steps, Billy stopped. Slowly turning around, he sat his grip down. These steps were one of the challenges here that he had never fully conquered. He remembered the first time he was able to jump upon the first step and then the second step and, quite a while later, the third step and finally the fourth step. But that left the fifth step. No matter how hard he tried or how often—and that was every day—he just couldn't reach the top of that step. One last try, one last time. He forgot about the Adamses. He forgot about the home. He forgot that he was leaving. He pushed his grip aside, slowly backing up to the right running distance, gently rocking back and forth on his feet. With his eyes riveted on that step, he took a deep breath then slowly let it out. Glancing up he said, "This is mine—you keep out of it." Taking one more deep breath, he took off, head back, arms pumping, oblivious to anything but the step high up in front of him. His right foot hit about three inches from the bottom step. He launched himself high and forward. It seemed like he was in the air forever, and he felt like he was in slow motion

BILLY YOU, NO MORE HILLS

as he watched that step coming down, down, and then it was below him and it was behind him. When he landed, he stood perfectly still for a few seconds, then twisting his body so as to see the steps behind him, he counted one, two, three, four, five. With that he let out a wild yell, jumping high in the air with his arm in the air and fist closed. That's when he remembered who he was and where he was at and who was waiting for him.

There they were, standing shoulder to shoulder with disapproving looks on their faces. Mr. Adams's hand was holding on to the wrought-iron gate post. All of a sudden it hit Billy, and he burst out laughing; now he knew why it was that he thought that he had known them from somewhere. They looked like the old farm couple he had seen in pictures and on TV. The man with a pitchfork in his hand, hair combed straight back and old-fashioned small round eyeglasses on; Mrs. Adams had her hair pulled back with a bun rolled up in back. Billy's laughter stopped as quick as it had started. Mr. Adams had taken a step forward with a mean look on his face.

Billy thought fast. "I'm sorry, sir, I wasn't laughing at you folks. It's just that I'm so happy to get out of this place. I had to jump up and down and holler and laugh."

That did it. Mr. Adams took his wife by the arm, saying, "Come on, get in the car, we've got a long way to go."

Chapter 2

Billy didn't glance heavenward to try and give some of the blame on you-know-who; the lie that he had told was all his own doing. He didn't feel a bit bad about telling it either. By the look on Mr. Adams's face, he felt that he had probably saved his life or, at least, saved himself from a bad beating.

The car was a dirty old station wagon. Billy was told to get in the backseat; he opened the door and came close to changing his mind about going. The seat and floor were covered with old newspapers, magazines, and empty soft drink bottles and cans. There were dirty, greasy rags—you name it; it was there. Billy went ahead, shoving the trash over so he would have enough room to sit. He lay his grip on top of the mess and settled in for the ride.

The Adamses didn't seem to be in any hurry. It was a narrow road through low rolling hills. After a while, Billy became drowsy. Twisting around, he lay down on his grip and dozed off. He didn't know how long he had slept, but when he woke up, the scenery had changed. Now they were driving alongside a fast-moving river, with the road running beneath some high rocky cliffs. On the other side of the river, it was all farmland with fresh-turned fields, some already starting to turn green; it was early spring. In a short while, the road turned, and they went over a bridge crossing the river. Now they were traveling down a farm road. With big two-storied houses scattered here and there, Billy thought to himself, *Someday I'll own a house like one of these.* After a while, they came to a wide place in the road, with a picnic table setting there.

Mr. Adams pulled in and said to Billy, "Get the lunch basket out of the back." Just like that, not "Would you get the lunch basket" but "Get the lunch basket." Billy was starting to have a little bit of dislike for this pair. He sat the basket on the table; Mrs. Adams opened it up. Taking out three sandwiches, she handed one to Billy, one to Mr. Adams, and kept one for herself. Then she took out two pint cartons of milk, setting one in front of Mr. Adams and herself. "I'm sorry, two milks is all I brought with us. There's some water in a jar in the car, you can have some of that."

Billy said, "Thank you, ma'am, this will do just fine." No way was he going to drink out of that jar. He had watched them both turn it up and drink out of it while they were traveling. He would go thirsty before he would drink after their slobber. Billy didn't wait for another order. He took the basket and put it in the station wagon.

Then the next order came, this one from Mrs. Adams. "Billy, before you get in, take these milk cartons and throw them in there. We don't want people to think that we're a bunch of pigs, do we?"

Billy wanted to say, "Ma'am, I don't think there's enough room back there for any more trash," but instead, he said, "Yes, ma'am."

As he was getting in the car, he looked heavenward, saying to himself, "They are not mine. They're yours. You created them." Back on the road, Billy dozed off again. He didn't know how long it was, but what woke him up was the most terrible noise he had ever heard in his life. He jumped straight up, banging his head on the car roof, looking around wildly for some place to escape to. Then he realized where he was; he was in the station wagon, still going down the road. Mr. Adams was still sitting behind the steering wheel, both hands gripping the steering wheel tight and staring straight ahead as if nothing was happening. Then the awful noise came again. Billy jerked his head around to where Mrs. Adams was sitting; she had slid down in the seat with her head over in the corner of the seat resting against the door. Her eyes were closed, and her mouth was wide open. Billy held his breath for that is what she seemed to be doing; she held it and held it. Then she sucked in a tremendous

CLARENCE W. LESLIE

amount of air—there was that god-awful noise—then as she let it out, it sounded like someone screaming in pain. He had heard some of the boys snore at the home, but that was nothing to what was going on here. If all the boys there snored as loud as they could at the same time, it would be no contest; the lady would beat them hands down. Billy looked over at Mr. Adams to see what he thought about all this noise. It didn't seem to be bothering him one bit. Both of his hands were on the steering wheel, and he was still staring straight ahead down the road like a zombie.

Billy put up with the noise as long as he could, but enough was enough. He tore a corner off an old newspaper lying in the trash heap. Rolling it up in a tight little ball, he eased back on his grip so as he could feign sleep if he woke her up. He didn't want to throw it for fear Mr. Adams would see the motion of his arm, so he gave it a flip with his thumb, like someone would shoot a marble. His aim was way off; he had planned on hitting her on the side of the head or her ear. The paper ball made a slow lazy arc, Billy believed if at that exact moment she hadn't taken one of the big deep sucking breaths, the ball might have gone right on by, but instead, it was like a vacuum cleaner sucking that paper ball right into her mouth and on down her throat. Billy had never seen such a violent reaction in all his life. She came alive with both feet kicking and both arms swinging, making wild strangling noises. One foot hit Mr. Adams in the head, driving his head and shoulder up against the closed window with a loud bang, causing Mr. Adams to jerk the steering wheel to the left. It was a good thing that there were no cars coming from the opposite direction; the station wagon shot across the center line. It kept on going over the other lane and on, bouncing and bumping down a low shoulder, coming to a skidding halt just before it hit a barbed wire fence guarding an alfalfa field.

Billy was thrown into the pile of garbage and trash in the floor. He came up clawing and scratching himself out of it, yelling, "What happened?" as if he didn't know a thing about what had taken place. The Adams were setting there staring at each other with their eyes and mouths wide open. Mr. Adams finally blurted out, "Woman, what in the hell came over you? Kicking me in the head like that?"

She grabbed her throat and started hacking and coughing, trying to clear her throat. "I was asleep. Something flew in my mouth— it was big, it was a bug or a fly or a bee. Oh my god! It was a bee. I bet it was a bee. It's in my throat—it's in there crawling around. Get me to a doctor. Hurry, you know what a bee sting does to me." She was starting to panic. "I'll swell up inside. I won't be able to breathe. Oh my god!"

Billy shook his head. Boy, she sure had that saying down good. She started hacking and coughing again. Then she screamed, "I got it, I got it." The wad of paper was in the palm of her hand; she held it up so as to get a better look.

"What is it?" She held it out for her husband to see. "What in the world is it?' He rolled it around in his hand with his finger with a puzzled look on his face. Billy leaned over the back of the seat saying. "What kind of a bee is it? Let me see."

Mr. Adams replied, "It's not a bee, I don't know what the darn thing is." He picked at the paper ball and pulled it apart. He looked at his wife with a question in his eyes. "It's a piece of paper." Billy jumped in, giving Mrs. Adams the same kind of look.

"A piece of paper?"

"Well, don't ask me how it got there. I was sound asleep when that spit wad fell into my mouth," Mrs. Adams said.

"Spit wad?" Billy sure wished she hadn't said that, for now they were both staring at him. It was time to tell another lie—two lies in one day, that was more lies than he had told in his whole life. He made his eyes look big and innocent.

"No, sir, No, ma'am, it wasn't me. I was asleep too. Why, sir, when you ran off the road it knocked me right down here between the seats. Sir, I was scared to death, I thought we were having a terrible wreck."

He was dragging it out too long. "Shut up, Billy you've told your lie, keep talking and you're going to blow it." His story must have satisfied them. Mr. Adams shoved the gear shift into reverse then punched the gas pedal; the car bounced up and down until the wheels got traction. then the station wagon shot back up the bank across the road and down the shoulder on the other side. Mr.

CLARENCE W. LESLIE

Adams uttered a bad oath and slammed the gear shift into forward at the same time, jamming the gas pedal hard. The station wagon went careening back up on the road. It came close to going back off the other side again, but Mr. Adams got control of the car in time to prevent it from happening. He headed on down the road, driving as he had been doing on the whole trip. Mrs. Adams sat there, staring straight ahead, as she had been doing before she had kicked Mr. Adams in the head, causing him to run off the road.

With Billy, it was a different story. It was a while before he could pull his feet back from where he had them pressed against the back of the front seat and release his fingers that were dug in a death grip into the car seat.

In just a few minutes, fifteen or less, they came over a low rise in the road, and there, nestled down below in a wide green valley, was a small village of no more than ten or twelve hundred people.

Mr. Adams didn't change speed as he drove into the town and down what appeared to be the main street. Mrs. Adams swiveled her head around to Billy. "We're here. This is our town, and now it's going to be your town. Mr. Adams and myself hope that you are going to live with us for a long time." With that, she gave him a big toothy smile. He had been thinking that she was a mite ugly, then she hit him with that smile; he felt that it went beyond ugly. If ugly hurt, this lady would be in a world of pain. With that thought in his head, he had to chuckle out loud, which made her smile grow all the wider, thinking that he was chuckling with happiness. Coming up on a Stop sign, Mr. Adams slowed up enough to make a right-hand turn. In the process, he cut a car off coming down the cross street. The car driver had to hit his brakes hard. He then gave a long protest blast on his home. In reply, Mr. Adams causally stuck his arm out the window and pointed his middle finger straight up, causing the other driver to blow his horn all the more.

Billy could not believe what was going on, especially the gesture that Mr. Adams had made with his finger. Pointing your finger like that at the boys in the home was an absolute no-no! Billy had found out the hard way. One of the older boys had yelled something at Billy that he hadn't liked, so Billy just up and flipped him off. What a mistake. A teacher that he hadn't known was anywhere around had taken hold of his wrist with one hand and the offending finger with the other. Holding his wrist firmly, she had bent his finger back. Billy could have sworn that it had touched the back of his hand. He had let out a yell of pain and went to the floor on his knees. Her face had come right down to his, eyeball to eyeball.

"Are you ever going to do a filthy thing like that again?"

"No, please, you're hurting me." She had given it another shove back, making Billy moan all the louder.

"Are you absolutely sure you're never going to do such a nasty thing again?"

"Yes, ma'am, yes, ma'am, please stop." Billy guessed that his whining and begging had paid off. She turned him loose and walked away, leaving him on the floor in pain, cussing under his breath as he held his damaged finger against his chest. A lot of the other boys had witnessed Billy's punishment, but not one of them laughed or made fun. That was another no-no! If you laughed at a boy being punished, you ended up getting the same treatment the boy being punished was getting.

As the station wagon came to the edge of town, Billy noted a big low building with a door at each end and one in the center of the building. He recognized it immediately as the school house. What gave him the clue that it was a school was out in the front were some swing sets and an open basketball court. Also there were a bunch of kids about his age and younger playing in the yard. There was no fence around the school, and in a part of the basketball court was a fairly deep wash or arroyo, as some people might call it. Over the wash was a bridge, where the road immediately began climbing up to a lone house setting on the side of a hill; it was the only building on that side of the wash. It looked like something the town didn't want and had moved it over there, out of the way.

Billy knew whose house it was, even before Mrs. Adams swirled her head around and hit him with that big toothy smile.

"We're home. This is our home. Now it's also your home for a long time." Still with that big smile on her face, she pointed back at the school saying, "And tomorrow you will be going to school right there."

Billy let out a protest, "Why tomorrow, why can't I wait until Monday?"

The teeth disappeared, and it was replaced by a heavy scowl. She aimed a finger at him with her thumb over the top of it like she was cocking a gun.

"Don't you ever talk back to me—*ever*, do you understand?"

Billy nodded his head. As an afterthought, she added, "And you will never talk back to Mr. Adams." Looking at her husband she asked, "Isn't that right?" Mr. Adams nodded his head. Billy assumed the head nod meant yes—that he, Billy, was never to talk back to Mr. Adams either. So he nodded his head in agreement. It looked to Billy like most of their conversations was going to be covered by head movements.

The station wagon pulled into a garage built under the house. Billy guessed it to be what you would call a split-level home.

The moment the car came to a stop, both front doors flew open. The husband-and-wife team charged a door going into the house from the garage like there was a dire emergency to get into the building. Mr. Adams, the last one through the door, yelled at Billy, "Bring the ice chest in." Billy didn't bother to reply; neither one of them could see him nor could they have heard him; the door had slammed shut behind them.

He did as he was told; with the ice chest in tow, he opened the door and stepped into the big clean kitchen. It startled him; no way had he expected to find something like this, based on the condition of the station wagon. It picked Billy's spirits up a dab. Bringing his grip in, he went through a door leading from the kitchen into a big clean living room. Billy's spirit jumped— another small dab—things were looking up somewhat.

The Adamses, the man-and-wife team, must have moved mighty fast after they entered the house, for they were sitting in big easy chairs drinking iced tea and watching a soap opera on TV. They were so deep into the show Billy was hesitant about breaking into their

BILLY YOU, NO MORE HILLS

concentration so as to find out where his bedroom was. Clearing his throat, he asked, "Ma'am, where will I be sleeping?"

Without taking her eyes off the TV, she pointed back over her head, saying, "Upstairs, there are two bedrooms. Take your pick." He hadn't noticed the stairway until she brought it to his attention. Going up, he found the two rooms, with a bathroom in between. Both rooms were small and neat, with a bed and dresser in each. He took the back one; he felt that there would be a little more privacy there.

Billy stayed in his room until evening. He had begun to think that there would be no evening meal. Then Mrs. Adams called up the stairway, "Supper's ready."

Billy felt that she could have said, "Billy, supper's ready, but what the heck." Down the stairs, he found the pair still sitting in their easy chairs, still watching TV, but now each had a tray sitting in their laps, with sandwiches and a glass of milk on each tray. He didn't bother to asking where his food was. Going into the kitchen, he found, sitting on the table, a dish full of sandwiches and a large glass of milk.

The next morning, Billy woke up early. He was excited, but he was also nervous. The home was the only school he had ever been to. Now he was starting on what he called his new school adventure.

Downstairs, he found it all quiet. The Adamses were nowhere in sight. On the table was a box of cold cereal, a big bowl, and a sugar jar. In the refrigerator sat a gallon of milk close to being empty, but there was enough for his cereal. He dallied around the house as long as he could, thinking of every excuse or reason that he shouldn't go to school.

The Adams hadn't made their appearance. So he grudgingly headed down the road and across the bridge, dragging his feet all the way. He very near panicked. The school yard was teaming with kids in various activities. They all stopped as if as one and stood staring at him, as he slowly made his way toward them.

He didn't roll his eyes up this time. He bent his neck back, and looking straight up, he said, "I don't know what I did to deserve all this that you have been handing down to me lately." He waited a few seconds, then said, "I didn't expect an answer, so I'll handle it myself." With that, he threw his shoulders back, and picking up the pace, he walked past the staring kids. There were three sets of steps leading up to the three doors. Steps at each end and one in the middle. He took the nearest one. Inside he stopped and stared around the place. There was a long hall running the entire length of the building. On his left were two doors. Above one it said *Girls*; above the other was the word *Boys*. That puzzled him for a moment, then it hit him—restrooms. In the home, there was no need for signs above the restroom doors; it was an all-boys' home. He moved down the hall. The first door he came to said, "1st, 2nd, and 3rd Grades." As he moved on, the next door said, "4th and 5th Grades." The third door said "6th," and the fourth and last door said "7th Grade" on it. He being in the seventh grade, this meant it was the door he was to enter.

At the end of the hall was another door and a big glass-plate window with big letters, spelling out *Principal* on it. It was a big clean room, and inside there was a big desk, and behind this desk sat a big man. A shiver went down Billy's back, for this big man with horn-rimmed glasses on was staring out at Billy the same way the kids in the school yard had. The difference was the kids had been watching him with curiosity. This man had a mean expression on his face and looked mad as heck. Billy quickly opened his door and stepped inside his new school room.

A tall slim blond-headed lady was standing in front of a blackboard, erasing some writing off the board as Billy came in. She stopped what she was doing. Placing the eraser down, she walked over to Billy, saying, "Good morning. You must be the young man staying with Mr. and Mrs. Adams."

Billy nodded. "Yes, ma'am."

Picking up some books that had been sitting on her desk, she said, "Follow me." Halfway down the middle aisle, she sat the books down. "This is your desk. The top lifts up, you will find—tablets, pencils, and notepads under there." Placing her hand on his shoulder, she said, "Welcome to our little school. It's nice to see a new face." It appeared as if she were going to say something else, but at that moment, the school room flew open and kids began streaming in.

Panic hit him again, and he seemed to freeze in place. As each boy and girl came through the door, their eyes darted in his direction. As the last ones filed in and settled into their desks, the teacher closed the door behind them. When the door slammed shut, Billy jumped and very nearly bolted. Gaining control of himself, he stood with his arms rigid at his sides.

There was a lot of bustling about, whispering, and settling in, then all was quiet. The tall blond teacher, standing up in front with a smile on her face, looked her class over. Then she gave out a cheery, "Good morning!"

The class returned the greeting, "Good morning, Mrs. Charles."

"Boys and girls, before we start classes, I want to introduce you to a new class member." Looking toward Billy and wiggling her finger at him, she said, "Would you please come up here?" He gave one last disappointed look at the door. Knowing it was hopeless, he squared his shoulders and marched up to where the teacher stood. As he turned around to face the class, a cold shiver went up his back. A sea of eyes was staring at him. He felt like a fish, standing there for them to gawk over.

Once again Mrs. Charles was speaking. "Please, I want each one of you to stand up one at a time, and introduce yourselves to our new friend." She pointed to the far row on her right. "We'll start with you, James." James was a tall, skinny kid. He stood, and stepping to the front of the row of desks, he said in a loud, arrogant voice, "My name is James McPherson Jr." with a big emphasis on the *Jr.* part. Billy realized who he was, for on the window at the end of the hall where it said *Principal* was also the lettering *James McPherson*. Billy listened as each boy and girl in turn stood up and stated their name, but none registered, until a small pretty redheaded girl sitting in a desk across from what was to be his desk stood up with a big smile he felt was meant for him and said, "Hi, my name is Mary McPherson, welcome to our school."

Billy's spirits jumped. The prettiest girl in school, he felt, had given him a smile and a welcome. The names came around until they reached the teacher. She said, "My name is Mrs. Charles." Then placing her hand on his shoulder, she said, "Now tell us your name."

CLARENCE W. LESLIE

Not one boy out there had said "My name is Billy." He would be the only Billy in class.

"My name is Billy," he said with pride.

A hush came over the kids as they all sat staring at him as if they were expecting something else, then from Mrs. Charles.

"And your last name?" That's when Billy's spirits that had soared when the redheaded girl named Mary had smiled and gave him a welcome hit rock bottom. Billy didn't have a last name. At the home they had called him Billy You. How that name came about: At one time, there were two boys in the home named Billy. One day, one of the matrons had screamed "Billy, come here this instant!" He knew which Billy she wanted, but instead of going to her, he shouted back, "Billy who?"

That really brought some anger into her voice.

"Billy you, that's who!" From that time on, he was known as Billy You.

And now the names were racing through his head as the room, in dead silence, waited for a last name from him. What name should he pick out to use? He rolled his eyes heavenward seeking help; no help came. Then he thought, *I've already told two lies since the Adamses picked me up, that's enough.*

"You, Billy You." The silence got deeper.

"Would you spell your last name, please?" This was from the teacher.

"Yes, ma'am, its spelled Y-o-u." The school came alive, came alive with laughter, with James leading the charge with a high-pitched braying laugh.

Billy hit him with the hardest look that he had, which made James bray all the louder. He turned to the boy in the desk behind him who was laughing just as loud. The two of them gave each other a high five. Those two were going to get the daylights punched out of them as soon as he could get to it. He ran his eyes over the rest of the room—they were laughing too, but it wasn't a make-fun-of-you laugh. The teacher was rapping on her desk, trying to get attention. The room slowly quieted down, with the tall skinny kid who was going to get his lights punched out giving a few last braying, hiccupping sounds.

Mrs. Charles, looking at Billy, said, "I'm sorry, there was absolutely no call for the class to act like that. I apologize for them and for myself."

Then with a smile on her face, she said, "You have to admit that's a very unusual name," looking back at him with a very solemn look.

"Yes, ma'am, I think I'm the only one in the world that has this name. That's why I chose it."

She had a confused look in her eyes. "I don't understand."

"I'm an orphan, and I picked my own name." That brought the room alive with dead silence.

Having dropped that bombshell, he walked back to his seat, glancing up. *How do you like the way I handled that? Didn't think I could do it, did you? Well, keep your eyes on me—you're going to see a lot of things I can do for myself. I may not need too much of your help anymore.* He immediately regretted saying it. He could use all the help he could get. His body had turned to jelly. The reason? Redheaded Mary had her big blue eyes on him, with the sweetest smile he had ever seen. Whispering, she said, "Welcome to our school. I'm sorry we laughed at you." He found his desk seat just in time to keep his knees from giving away and his body melting down to the floor.

She was still smiling at him; it had been a long time since he had smiled. He smiled back, which made her smile grow wider, which made his smile grow wider, which made her smile grow wider. If Mrs. Charles hadn't called the class to order right then, no telling how wide their smiles would have grown.

Mrs. Charles was talking. "James, will you pass the test sheets out, please?" Turning her attention to Billy, she said, "Billy, each morning, we start our day with a test on subjects that were studied the week before. Today our test will be arithmetic. Now since you didn't have the opportunity to study with us last week, in all fairness to you, we won't grade your test this morning." Then she smiled sweetly at him. "OK?"

"Yes, ma'am."

CLARENCE W. LESLIE

James had been passing out the test papers as Mrs. Charles had been talking, laying a test paper on each desk. Now reaching Billy's desk, he very slowly and carefully placed the sheet on the edge of the desk, where it slid off and went floating down to the floor. The skinny boy didn't stop to pick it up or say "I'm sorry." He went on about his business, handing out the papers. Billy mentally put another check mark against James's name; that was one more punch he was going to give that boy, as he punched his lights out.

Reaching down to get the paper, his hand came in contact with Redheaded Mary's hand, causing him to jerk back as if he had touched a rattlesnake. He had never in his life had any contact with a girl, and he didn't know how he was supposed to react. Redheaded Mary giggled as she handed him the paper. Billy was blushing, but beet-red, he was glad to hear Mrs. Charles speaking again. "Class, you have twenty minutes to complete your test. As each of you finish, very quietly, so as not to disturb the others that are still working, bring your paper to my desk. Then open your math book to page 194, chapter 12, and begin studying."

Picking up what Billy assumed was a timer, she pushed some buttons on it, then looking the room over, she said, "Start."

Chapter 3

Billy, as he looked at his test paper, could hear other students shuffling their papers around, preparing to answer the test questions. A smile lit up his face. The math test in front of him was what the home had taught them the year before. He might not have a last name, as the other kids in school did, which had made him feel bad. Well, now he was going to turn the tables. They could have their names; he was going to show them who had the brains. Very near as fast as he could write, he filled the answers in. Standing up, he stood by his desk for a moment, waiting some of the other kids to notice that he had finished the test. Walking slowly up the aisle so as to attract more attention, he handed the paper to the waiting Mrs. Charles, who had a smile on her face that said, "That's all right, we didn't expect you to do the math test, without studying it."

Back at his desk, he sat down and glanced at Mrs. Charles and returned the smile she had given him a while ago. He hadn't really meant for it to be a smug smile, but that's the way it came out. As for Mrs. Charles, she was looking at him with a startled look on her face, and Billy thought her mouth was hanging open just a speck.

He felt good. They may all have their last names; he's the one that had the brain. After the last kid had handed in his test sheet, Mrs. Charles went to the blackboard at the back of her desk. Picking up a piece of chalk, she wrote a math problem down. Turning and looking the class over, she pointed at James and said, "Would you come up here and work this math problem for us?"

The tall boy that was going to get his lights punched out strutted up to the blackboard. It took him a while, but he got the correct answer.

The teacher told him, "Very good, James," as he strutted back to his desk. Mrs. Charles went through the same process with two of the other classmates. One of them, a big heavy boy, struggled with the problem, but with a little coaching from the teacher, he got the right answer. Then, looking his way, she asked, "Billy, would you mind coming up here and doing this one?"

He stood up. "No, ma'am, I wouldn't mind doing it." A titter of giggles went through the room. Billy thought to himself, *All these kids should have to spend some time at the home. There you were taught that when someone asked you a question, you answered them back, and you answered them very politely.*

Now as he went toward the blackboard, he was doing his version of the strut. He didn't like to think that he was; he felt that he had a reason to strut. The math questions Mrs. Charles had put on the blackboard he had been able to answer in his head before the students could write the correct answer down.

He took his time going to the blackboard. Not one time did he glance at the math question written up there for him to solve. As he passed the teacher, he gave her a smile; she smiled back. Billy picked up the chalk. Getting a little chalk dust on his fingers, he took a little more time to wipe it on his pants. Then quickly he looked up and wrote the answer down without ever looking at the problem. There was dead silence in the room as he did the double strut back to his desk.

Redheaded Mary had a hand over her mouth, trying to hold back a giggle, then she closed one eyelid over one of her pretty eyes. It hit Billy like a bolt of lightning! That he had just been winked at. The strut left his legs. He quickly sat down, thankful for his desk; this was the second time the desk had saved him. Billy didn't know what love felt like but thought that he might have it. Right then and there, Billy changed his mind. All the other kids should have to go to the home for proper training, but not Redheaded Mary.

Billy thought of her as Redheaded Mary. No way could he think of her as just a girl named Mary.

All the other classes were just as easy for him as the math class had been.

The weekend came and went.

The weather became warmer each passing day. School would soon be out. Billy didn't like the thought of it.

At school, he could see and talk to Redheaded Mary. When school let out for the summer break, he probably wouldn't get to see her again until the fall of the year.

The rest of the kids at school were starting to accept him, with the exception of James. He went out of his way to be rude to Billy, making fun of his name and the fact that he was an orphan.

Billy kept his temper under control. No way did he want the redheaded girl to get mad at him because he had punched her brother's lights out. But Redheaded Mary was his downfall. She noticed that Billy never brought dessert in his lunch, so she began bringing dessert for him. If she had six cookies, three were for him; if she had cake, there was a piece for him, the same with pie. They always sat together at lunchtime. She never stopped talking, and he never stopped listening. This was the happiest he had ever been in his whole life. He wasn't mad anymore at the Adamses for bringing him here. Redheaded Mary had just handed him a big slice of chocolate cake. He put it up to his mouth ready to take a big bite; at that moment, James walked by. Reaching down, he slapped the back of Billy's head, smashing the cake all over Billy's face. Billy stood up, then he brushed the cake off his face and hands. On the way to the bathroom to clean up, he looked up. "You see how much patience I've had with James? Just now he pushed it past the breaking point. I don't want you taking his side when I get back out there and punch his lights out."

Billy could hear some of the kids laughing as the school door closed behind him. He took his time cleaning up. Going back outside, he stopped on the top step. He looked over to where James and his buddy were standing. When they saw Billy come out onto the steps, they began laughing again and pointing at him. Redheaded

Mary was looking at him, her eyes big and round. He thought there was a frightened expression on her face. The rest of the kids in the school yard were all moving closer, as if they were expecting something dramatic to happen.

Billy stood where he was for a while longer. He wanted to be sure they were all there to see him punch James' lights out; he might even dim James's buddy's light at the same time.

Billy came down the steps and walked toward James until he was face-to-face with him. James said, "You looked better with the cake on your face." Throwing his head back, he gave that long, braying laugh. Some of the other kids joined in but not many of them. In the home, it became the practice that if you wanted to pick a fight, you would flip the other boy on the nose with your finger. That's what Billy did to James. James, letting out a yell of anger, took a wild swing at Billy's head. Billy ducked the punch, and there was James's nose standing out like a big target. Billy smashed it with his left fist; the target spewed blood. He started to punch the nose again, but there was no need to. James, with his hand up to his face, took off running and crying toward the school building. Now it was his turn to wash his face. The rest of the kids were staring at Billy with awe on their faces. Then one of the boys let out a wild whoop. "Yeah, Billy." With that, all the kids began cheering and hollering. He glanced at Redheaded Mary; her eyes were wide with fright.

Just then the bell rang, summoning them back to the school rooms. As Billy was going up the steps, the redheaded girl caught up with him and grabbed hold of his arm, saying, "Billy, I'm afraid!"

He looked at her and asked, "Afraid of what?"

"I'm not afraid for me. I'm afraid for you. Daddy might do something terrible."

"James started it."

"I know, but Daddy will believe anything my brother tells him, and James is a big spoiled brat, and he's Daddy's pet." By this time they were in the classroom. Billy went to his desk, sitting down with a small amount of apprehension. The door to the room slammed open. James came charging in; the blood was gone, but his nose was swollen and red.

BILLY YOU, NO MORE HILLS

Mrs. Charles asked him, "James, what in the world happened to you?"

James pointed to Billy and screamed, "That no-name Billy hit me."

Mrs. Charles with a question in her voice, said, "Billy!"

Before Billy could speak, Mr. McPherson came charging in faster than his son had, and like his son, he pointed at Billy and screamed, "You come here."

He heard Redheaded Mary in a pleading voice softly say, "Oh no!" Standing up, she said, "Daddy, please." Moving his pointing finger from Billy to his daughter, he said, "I'll take care of you later." The deadly looking finger swept back toward Billy. "You come here or I'll come down there and take hold of your dirty neck and drag you out of here."

Billy wanted to stand up and say, "Sir, you know my name real good. You have called me You enough times."

Then all of a sudden he was scared; he had never seen a look on any face like the one he was seeing now, on Mr. McPherson's face. Quickly he got up and went toward the pointing finger. He thought he heard the redheaded girl start to cry. Mrs. Charles gave him a look of what he thought was pity. What the heck—he had been spanked before; he would show them that he was just as tough as he was smart.

He followed Mr. McPherson out of the room. From there it was just a few steps to the principal's office. Once he was inside, he was told to "Shut the door."

Billy, saying "Yes, sir'," shut the door. All of a sudden, a cold chill ran down his back. He felt as if he was trapped in this room with something that was very evil. For a while, the principal stood with his back to Billy, staring at the wall in front of him. The longer he stood that way, the more nervous Billy became. Then he whirled around with that deadly pointing finger which made Billy cringe back a step.

"The minute I heard that this school was going to have to take in a kid like you, I knew we were going to have a problem."

"Sir, your son started it." The slap came so hard and fast he didn't see it coming. It caught him on the side of the head, knocking him sideways. If the big desk that was sitting there had not been sitting there for him to grab hold of, he would have hit the floor. With fear creeping into his body but still defiant, he pushed himself, ringing head and all, away from the desk. "Sir, your son smashed cake all over my face, then hit at me first."

Mr. McPherson went livid; he drew back his fist as if to hit Billy. Billy put up his arms in protection. The principal didn't follow through. Instead he began looking frantically around as if he had lost something; his eyes fell on Billy's belt.

With that pointing finger, he said, "Take that fancy belt off and hand it to me."

Billy was proud of his belt. A few months back, the home had taken the boys in Billy's age group to a big farm not far from the home. While wandering around, Billy had noticed an old set of harnesses hanging on the barn wall. It had brass ornaments. The ornaments were half round, about the size of a small marble that had been cut in half. As Billy had looked at them, the old farmer walked in, asking, "Would you like those beads?"

The farmer took a piece of the harness down. Handing it to Billy, he said, "Here, you can have this. I'll never use something like this again."

Billy's eyes lit up; he could already see what they would like on his belt.

"Wow. Thank you, sir." Billy was the first one off the bus as it came to a stop back at the home.

Rushing into the kitchen, he asked Mr. Cook if he could borrow a knife, telling the cook what he wanted it for. Mr. Cook sat down and helped him; on the back side of the harness, there were two flanges bent over. Mr. Cook bent them back straight and popped the bead off the harness. They took all the beads off, then they punched holes in a zigzag pattern and fit the brass beads to Billy's belt. This was the belt Billy was proud of.

Now Mr. McPherson wanted that belt, and Billy knew why. At the home, when they spanked you or twisted your ear or rapped you on the knuckles, it was just a gentle reminder to stop what you were doing. As Billy handed his belt to the principal, he knew this was going to be terribly different.

Mr. McPherson told him to put his hands on the desk and lean forward. Gritting his teeth, Billy did as he was told. He heard the swish of the belt as the principal brought it down in a hard, furious swing, Billy held back a cry of pain as he felt those brass ornaments dig into his body. He closed his eyes and hung on as the principal steered the punishment; each blow seemed more painful than the one before.

After giving Billy eight or nine hard licks, Mr. McPherson took hold of Billy's arm and pulled him up straight. He bent down and yelled in Billy's face, "You think this is going to teach you some manners?"

Answering, Billy said, "Yes, sir, I guess it will."

The second he put the word *guess* in there, Billy knew he had made a terrible mistake. The principal's face turned purple with rage. Still retaining a hold on Billy's arm, he slammed him across the desk. Billy put out his hands, trying to stop himself. The desktop was too slick; his hands went sliding across the surface. Mr. McPherson went into a frenzy before Billy could push himself up off the desk. The first blow of the belt hit him across the middle of the back; it knocked a grunt of pain out of him. Billy begged, "Please stop, please stop. I didn't mean it that way." His voice was drowned out by Mr. McPherson's, screaming, "You guess that's enough, you guess that's enough!" With each screaming word, the belt came slashing down across the small of Billy's back; he lost count of the blows.

Things were beginning to get hazy; he no longer felt the pain, just the blows. He didn't realize the beating had stopped until from a long way off, he heard the principal shouting at him, "Answer me when I talk to you. I asked if you guessed that this was enough?"

Billy gasped out, "Yes, sir'.' He didn't recognize his voice; it sounded as if someone had his head hanging down inside a barrel as he talked. Billy was standing up now and trying to get Mr. McPherson in focus.

The principal was telling him something. "If you ever lay a hand on my son again, you will dearly regret it."

Billy mumbled a "Yes, sir."

Throwing the belt onto the floor, he said, "Pick that up, and get out of here." As Billy bent over to take the belt off the floor, the room began spinning. He had to grab hold of the desk edge and drop to one knee. Coming up with the belt in hand, he moved toward the door, taking slow deliberate steps. The doorknob seemed to elude his trembling hand. Finally, as he stepped out into the hall, he heard Mr. McPherson say, "And stay away from my daughter, I don't want you near her."

Chapter 4

The hall looked like a long narrow tunnel and seemed to be a mile long as he began the long journey down it.

He tried to remember if he had answered the principal when he warned him to stay away from the redheaded girl. He must have, or Mr. McPherson would have been pointing the finger and shouting at him.

He made it to the far door, using the wall for support by placing his hand there to steady himself when he would feel a dizzy spell coming on. Outside, standing on the top step, he began to feel better. He stayed there a while, letting the cool breeze blow over his face. He worked his way down the steps, using the hand rail to balance himself.

Once on the school yard ground, he picked up his pace; he had lost all track of time. He was afraid the school would let out, and he didn't want any of them to see the condition he was in. About then, he felt that there was something wrong. Glancing down, he saw that the front of his pants was wet. He tried to get his legs to move into a run, as he looked back over his shoulder in shame. He had wet his pants, and he never knew when he had done it.

His legs didn't respond to the signal to run, but his stumbling walk picked up more speed. He was terrified that the other kids would come out and see his wet pants. He reached the bridge, then he was across it, going up the rise to the house; that's when the pain hit him. His lower back and hips felt like they had caught on fire.

Inside the house, he found Mr. Adams stretched back in his recliner chair sound asleep. Mrs. Adams was sitting in her chair engrossed in one of her soap operas. Billy slipped quietly up the stairs without either of them knowing that he was home.

In his room, he gingerly took his clothes off. The back of his undershirt was covered with blood. His undershorts were wet, which caused shame to rush over him again, but there were just a few specks of blood. Going down the hall to the shower, he turned the water to lukewarm. Stepping under it, he was surprised it didn't hurt him as bad as he thought it would. After standing under the water at that temperature for a while, he turned it down to cold; a few quick breaths were all he could take of that.

Out of the shower, he dried all of his body off except his back and backside. He let the towel drape over that part of him until he was dry. Putting on fresh undershorts, he took the bloody clothes and washed them in the bathroom sink, then hung them on the towel rack to dry. Now he felt weak and exhausted, and his back still hurt. Going to his bed, he lay down on his side and pulled a sheet up over himself, hoping that he wouldn't get blood on it. The next thing he knew, Mrs. Adams was shaking him and telling him to wake up. The first thought that entered his head was that he had overslept and was going to be late for school. He tried to sit up, but the pain in his back forced him back down. Mrs. Adams was talking to him. "Billy, are you sick?"

He didn't want her to know what had happened at school, so he told her a lie. Telling lies seemed to be getting into a habit with him, he thought.

"Yes, ma'am, I wasn't feeling good, so my teacher sent me home." She patted him on the shoulder. "You just stay right here in bed, and I'll bring you a big bowl of soup."

"Thank you, ma'am." With the soup, she also brought two slices of buttered toast.

Mr. McPherson had taken Billy into his office on a Thursday, and there was no way that Billy could get up and go to school on Friday. He had trouble just getting out of bed to go to the bathroom. Mrs. Adams was nicer than he could have ever imagined she would

BILLY YOU, NO MORE HILLS

be. Friday morning she brought him a big breakfast, with a glass of water and two aspirins. He wanted to go downstairs for lunch, but she would have none of that. She served him lunch and the evening meal in bed.

Saturday he felt much better, so he went downstairs for his meals. Other than that, he stayed in his room, lying on the bed, dozing. If he wasn't on the bed, he would be staring out the window. His mind felt like an open hole that no thought would stay in. He would be thinking of something that had happened in the home, then before he finished the thought, his mind would go blank, and he would find himself staring out the window at nothing.

Sunday was somewhat better; Mr. and Mrs. Adams went for a Sunday drive. They asked him if he wanted to go along. He told them, "No, thank you"; he didn't feel like it, but it was awful nice of them to ask.

He spent the day pacing the floor, dreading the thought that he had to go to school and face the kids. By now they all knew what had happened to him after the principal had removed him from the school room. As hard as he willed it, Billy couldn't stop Monday morning from coming.

It came bright and clear. A beautiful spring day. He fixed himself a big bowl of oatmeal, which he ate without tasting. Then with dragging feet he went to meet—he didn't know what. There were a few kids playing in the school yard. They stopped to gawk at him as he hurried on past them and up the steps into the schoolhouse.

For the first time in his life Billy felt pure panic. Down at the end of that long hall, sitting at his desk, was Mr. McPherson. His unblinking eyes were riveted on Billy. All of Billy's instincts said "Turn and flee," but Billy knew that if he gave into his fear, the principal would have another victory over him, and he would never be able to live with himself again. So with trembling legs, he traversed what seemed to him an endless hallway, with the principal's eyes glued to him every step of the way. And what was bad was Billy couldn't pull his eyes away from those eyes that he felt he was being drawn right into. What seemed like an eternity later, Billy's fumbling hand found the doorknob that let him escape into the safe way of his school room.

The only person in the room was Mrs. Charles, who was sitting behind her desk, grading test papers. When she saw who it was that had entered the room, she stopped grading the test papers and hustled over to Billy. Placing a hand on one of his shoulders, she looked into his eyes. "Billy, are you all right?"

"Yes, I'm fine."

"Are you sure?"

"Yes, ma'am, I have never felt better in my whole life." He had told so many lies in the last couple of weeks he felt one more wouldn't make any difference this late in life.

There was doubt in her eyes as she still looked into his eyes. With a pat on the shoulder and in a very soft voice she said, "It's nice to have you back, Billy."

"Thank you, ma'am."

Going to his desk, he sat down. With bated breath he waited for the other kids to come pouring in.

When the bell began clanging, calling the students to their classrooms, Billy came close to bolting out of the building. It took all his willpower to stay put, but to his surprise, nothing shattering happened. A few of the kids glanced his way, but the majority of them went about the business of settling into their desk seats. About then, Billy's heart jumped right up into his throat and stopped beating—or so it felt to Billy.

Redheaded Mary had just entered the room. With head down, she marched past the rows of desks. As she reached the aisle where Billy was sitting, she tilted her head ever so slightly in his direction and wiggled her fingers at him, which caused his heart to bounce around inside like a butterfly. Then it sank like a rock to the bottom of his stomach. The redhead girl walked right on past and on to the last row of desks and settled into a desk there. Billy was destitute. A chubby good-natured kid named Ron came and sat at Mary's old desk. Depression sat in as Billy withdrew into himself. He would sit with folded hands, staring down at the desktop with his books unopened. When the test papers were handed out, he would answer the questions, and quietly, looking neither left or right, he would go up and place the paper on the teacher's desk, never looking at her. He never knew how many times Redheaded Mary's eyes would drift his way with sadness in them. Or how many times Mrs. Charles would be watching him with concern in her eyes. All Billy could think about was the beating Mr. McPherson had given him and the humiliation he had been put through. The week slipped past, and thankfully, the weekend was here.

Chapter 5

The weather was warm, and it felt good on Billy as he went hiking among the trees and bushes above the Adamses' home. On Sunday they asked him if he wanted to go to church with them. He declined; some of the kids from school would be there, and he didn't like the thought of having to face them. Being associated with them on a school day was all that he felt he needed. After taking his hike, he made himself some lunch.

Still restless, he wandered around the house. Going into the garage, he spied what appeared to be a plastic frog or toad lying on its side up on a shelf at the end of the building. Taking it down from the shelf, he found that the frog had a spring on the bottom of it. Sitting the plastic toy down on the garage floor, he compressed it; the frog jumped high into the air. As it came down, it landed back on the spring and launched itself back in the air. It did this four or five times, hopping across the floor; each bound was shorter than the previous one. Finally it came to a stop; it swayed back and forth then fell over onto its side. Billy played with the toy for a short while, then as he was placing it back on the shelf from where he found it, an image of the principal popped into his head. On each Tuesday of the week, at the start of class, the principal would enter the room, and he always carried a black briefcase. With great pomp and show, he would set the briefcase on Mrs. Charles's desk and unsnap the latches, then before lifting the lid, he would, with a smug smile of self-appreciation on his face, look the class over and say, "My, what

BILLY YOU, NO MORE HILLS

a fine group of boys and girls we have here this morning." Then with a great show of importance, he would raise the lid, swinging his arms wide, and stare into the briefcase as if he had some fabulous treasure in there. Waiting for a moment for the suspense to build up, he would reach in and pull out a small newspaper clipping or some notes he had made for himself, then trying to bring his voice down an octave or two so as to sound more manly, he would read the clipping or notes, which everyone happened to have, on that particular Tuesday morning.

It was usually about drugs or drinking or smoking; then he would go into a long boring tirade of these and other sinful traps that kids could fall into in these days and times.

That was the image that popped into Billy's head. The next image that entered Billy's head was this frog toy here springing up in the principal's face one of these times when he opened the briefcase in front of the class. The thought of that caused Billy to start laughing, and the more he thought about it, the harder he laughed. After he had finally gotten his laughter under control, he felt much better about himself. But Monday morning, on the way to school, apprehension began to creep back in, and by the time he had crossed the bridge and entered the school yard, all the old self-doubts and uncertainties had taken hold of him again. With head down, he hurried past the kids playing in the school yard. Instead of going up the first set of stairs, as he usually did, he went up the third and last set. This way he wouldn't have to walk that long hallway with the principal's eyes on him every step of the way. At the top of the stairs he hesitated. All that he had to do was step through the open door, walk the few short steps across the hall and into his classroom. Inhaling a deep breath of air, he entered the building. With all the power he had, he willed himself not to look to his right, where he knew Mr. McPherson would be sitting, behind his desk. It was no use; there seemed to be a power stronger than his.

It pulled his head around, and he was staring into the hate-filled eyes of the principal. Once more, Billy felt fear taking hold of him, as with legs that felt like stilts he stumbled across the hall and into the sanctuary of the classroom. Closing the door, he leaned back against it, as humiliation engulfed him. The ringing of the bell helped pull him out of it. He hurried to his desk and was sitting there as the rest of the students came filing in. The morning slipped past, and it was recess time.

Billy sat where he was as the other kids went charging out to try and get as much playing time in as they could in the fifteen minutes' allotted time they had coming.

Mrs. Charles looked up from her paper work. Upon seeing that Billy was sitting there, she slowly got up from her desk. Going over, she closed the door that the departing students had left open. After doing that, she came down the row of desk where he was still sitting. She sat down sideways in the desk across from him so that she would be facing him. Then in a really soft voice, she asked, "Billy, what did Mr. McPherson do to you that day he took you from the class room to his office?"

With hands folded on his desk, he answered in a voice so low she could barely hear him. "He whipped me."

"How did he whip you?"

"He just whipped me."

This time there was some aggravation in her tone. "Billy, look at me when I talk to you."

With an effort, Billy turned his head so that the teacher could look into his eyes.

"Now tell me what really happened in there."

"He beat me! He beat me! He beat me!" To Billy her eyes seemed to mist up.

"It was terrible, wasn't it?" Billy stared at his folded hands for long moments. "He shamed me."

Mrs. Charles stood up. Taking a hold of his shoulder, she twisted him so that he was facing her. "Look at me, Billy."

Slowly he did. "He didn't shame you, he shamed himself. 'Now you quit feeling sorry for yourself. Billy, I've been so proud of you. A little boy that never had parents or family to help guide you, yet you seemed so sure of yourself. You walked with your head so high and your shoulders square, and no matter who it was, you looked them right in the eye with pride."

BILLY YOU, NO MORE HILLS

Still staring into his eyes, she told him, "Billy, I would like to see you get that pride back. Would you do it for me, please?"

With just those few words from the teacher, Billy began feeling better about himself; he felt new life pumping into his body. Sitting up with his shoulders back, he looked straight into the teacher's questioning eyes, and in a firm, sure voice, he answered, "Yes, ma'am!!"

Billy went through the rest of the day feeling good about himself; his old reassurance was back. Then at lunchtime, his spirits got a tremendous boost. Billy always waited for the other kids to leave the room, then he would follow the last one out.

Today he noticed out of the corner of his eye that Redheaded Mary was taking her time as she arranged some papers on her desk. The minute Billy moved up the aisle, the redheaded girl stopped fussing with the papers on her desk and intercepted Billy before he reached the door. He had tried to pick up his pace so as to get out the door so that he wouldn't have to face her.

"Billy." Her voice stopped him dead in his tracks. Taking a hold of his arm and looking into his face, she said, "Billy I'm ashamed for what my brother and father did to you, but please don't be mad at me." Then before he had a chance to say he wasn't mad at her, she rose up on her tiptoes and kissed him square on the lips. Having done that, she darted around him and went flying out the door.

If anyone would have entered the school at that instant, they would have thought Billy had been hit by a bolt of lightning or had been frozen in place. Billy stood there stunned, no part of his body moving but his heart, and it was doing cartwheels inside his chest.

After long moments, he willed his legs to move him out the door and down the hall to his locker from which he took his lunch sack. Moving on outside, he sat down in a nice sunny spot, as close to the redheaded girl as he dared to get without upsetting her father. As he opened up his lunch and looked inside, he got hit with another jolt—there, lying on top of his sandwich, was a big piece of chocolate cake. He jerked his head up, and there was Redheaded Mary watching him with a smile on her lips, then she lowered one of her eyelids down over one of her big pretty eyes, hitting Billy with another one of her winks.

CLARENCE W. LESLIE

Billy had thought that maybe he was in love; now there was no doubt in his mind. He was head over heels in love with this red-headed girl. The rest of the day went by in a blur for Billy, and on the way home, he was walking on air.

The next morning, Billy fixed his breakfast then packed his lunch; with lunch sack in hand he went out the kitchen door into the garage. As he stepped into the garage, out of the corner of his eye, he spied the toy frog lying there on the shelf. His brain told him no, but Billy didn't listen. Taking the frog down, he found that it would not fit in his lunch bag. Rushing back into the house, he found a larger paper bag, a grocery sack; there was plenty of room in this for both, his lunch and the frog.

There was just three more weeks of school, counting this week, so Billy didn't know if he would get the opportunity to place the frog in the principal's briefcase or not. Upon entering the school yard, his heart gave a jump. There, over at the only basketball court in the school yard, was Mr. McPherson playing basketball with his son and his son's shadow. Sitting around on the ground with sullen looks on their faces were some of the other boys hoping the principal would leave so that they could shoot a few baskets before they had to go into their classes.

And there on the far set of steps all the teachers sat, having their morning coffee and tea, enjoying the sun on this beautiful Tuesday morning. Entering the building, there was nobody in sight. Billy sprinted the length of the hallway.

The principal's office was unlocked. Quickly entering, Billy saw the briefcase sitting on the desk.

Sitting the sack down, he flipped the latches and opened the briefcase. Sure enough, lying in there were some newspaper clippings. Removing the plastic frog from the bag, he sat it on top of the clippings then slowly closed the lid so the frog wouldn't fall over. Snapping the latches shut, he grabbed his paper sack. Easing through the door, he closed it gently behind him. Billy sprinted back down the hall to his locker, in which he placed his lunch.

Wadding up the sack—he had the toy in—he placed it in a trash can that was sitting nearby. Now as he casually walked down to

BILLY YOU, NO MORE HILLS

the far door and out, he felt doubt starting to slip in, but it was too late to do anything about it; the deed was done. He mingled with the other kids until the bell called them in.

He felt a small twinge of apprehension; he remembered reading something about the tolling of the bells. He wondered as he listened to the school bell ring if it was tolling for him.

Billy knew by the fact that Mrs. Charles hadn't moved behind her desk to be ready to greet her students after they had all settled in and became silent that the principal would be here this morning.

Then as if on cue, the door swung open, and Mr. McPherson came striding in. He swung the door shut behind him with a loud bang, as if he were announcing his arrival. He moved around behind Mrs. Charles's desk; he took her chair. The chair had rollers on it, and it rolled back a ways. Putting his briefcase on the desk, he placed his hands on it with his fingers spread wide. Then looking the students over with a big toothy smile, he spoke.

"My, what a fine looking group of boys and girls we have here this morning." He stood that way for a moment, letting them admire his teeth and charm.

Then Billy looked on with bated breath as Mr. McPherson's long thumbs snaked down and unhooked the briefcase latches. Running his self-appraising smile over his audience, he hesitated a moment, then with a flourish, he raised the lid up, throwing his arms wide as if expecting applause. Instead he got that plastic frog; it came springing up out of that briefcase, right at the principal's face. He let out a wild shriek, the kind that Billy felt a woman should make, not a man.

Mr. McPherson jumped backward, his arms still spread wide. The back of his legs hit Mrs. Charles's chair, which caused him to keep going over, taking the chair with him as he hit the floor. The chair shot from under him, and if Mrs. Charles hadn't been fleet of foot, the charging chair may have nailed her.

Now the principal was lying flat on his back on the floor. After the frog had made its initial jump out of the briefcase, it had come down, hitting the corner of the desk, which caused it to bound high back into the air and, now, to Mr. McPherson's horrified eyes, was coming down as if it was going to attract his face. He let out a pitiful squeak and began scooting along on his back like a crab, propelling himself along with his heels and elbows. The frog hit a few inches from his face with a sponging sound, which was drowned out by another wild squeak from the principal.

By now the kids were all jumping up and down, drowning out the principal's shrieks with their shrieking laughter.

By now Billy knew that he had made the biggest goof of his life. His eyes darted toward Mrs. Charles; she had both hands over her mouth, holding back laughter. His eyes jumped to Redheaded Mary; she was jumping up and down screaming with laughter, and she wasn't trying to hide it. Next he swiveled his head so as to see James. There was a different story here—the boy was standing in stunned silence with his mouth hanging open, staring in disbelief at the antics his father was doing on the floor.

The frog was just about finished; it made one feeble effort to get back in the air but failed. It sat there rocking back and forth on its spring then slowly fell over on its side and lay still.

Mr. McPherson rolled over and came up on his hands and knees. He stared at the harmless toy for long minutes.

Then taking a hold of the frog, he slowly and deliberately stood up. His shirttail was hanging out of his pants, his hair was messed up, and the back of his shirt and pants were soiled from scooting across the floor. The kids had stopped laughing and were sitting straight and stiff in their seats.

Billy thought that he had never seen so much rage and embarrassment on a person's face in his entire life as he sat with his eyes riveted on the principal standing in front of the class. He stood there for a long time with what seemed to be a death grip on that toy frog, as he tried to gain control of his emotions. Then his arm shot out with, as Billy saw it, that deadly pointing finger.

It was aimed first at the far side of the room, then began a slow arc across the students shocked faces. You could see each kid flinch as that finger seemed to touch them. Then you could see the relief in their eyes as it swept on past. When the finger reached Billy, it came to a quivering halt, like a bird dog that had just picked up the scent of its prey. "You little bastard," came the screaming voice behind the finger.

Fear hit Billy so hard he came close to wetting his pants again. At the same time, he thought, *Mister, if you said a curse word like that at the home, you would be made to sit in a chair and eat a bar of soap with the rest of the boys looking on.*

The principal took a step or two in Billy's direction, the pointing finger began beckoning. With his brain racing a mile a minute, Billy stood up. As he did, he cocked his eyes heavenward, saying to God under his breath, "I could sure use some help right about now." Not really expecting a reply, Billy, on hesitant legs and dragging feet, moved toward the principal. There was no way he would take another beating like the principal had administered to him the last time.

Not liking the slow progress Billy was making, Mr. McPherson charged down between the rows of desks to meet him. Grabbing hold of Billy's arm with a grip that made Billy flinch, he stooped down and hissed in his ear, "You little son of a bitch, you didn't learn your lesson, did you? Well, you're going to regret the day you embarrassed me in front of the class."

Having said that, the principal marched back past the row of desks and headed for the door, dragging Billy along with him. Before they reached the door, Redheaded Mary came running and blocked the door. Looking up into her father's face, she pleaded, "Daddy, please don't do this, please." Billy felt a flash of hope, but it was quickly shattered. The father's reply to his daughter was a sharp slap to her face. Then in that hissing voice that he had used on Billy, he told her, "Get back to your desk, young lady, we'll finish this at home."

Billy could see some of the fear that she felt in her eyes. With her hand to her stinging cheek, she backed away from her father. Looking at Billy, she mouthed, "I'm sorry."

In reply, he threw back his shoulders and gave her a big reassuring wink to let her know that everything was all right, but inside he knew that everything was all wrong. Somehow he had to get away from the principal, and it wouldn't do to just get away for today. He had to get back to the boys' home. He knew that it would upset Mrs. Jamison, but it was possible that after he explained to her and showed her the scars on his back, she would understand.

Then Mrs. Charles gave Billy his opening. She said, "Mr. McPherson, we don't know for sure if Billy did this. It could have been someone else. let's all cool down and think about it."

This time, the pointing finger was aimed at the teacher. "You open your mouth one more time, and by God, you won't be teaching school here tomorrow." To place a bigger emphasis on his words, he took a step toward Mrs. Charles. In doing this, he loosened his grip on Billy's arm. That was the break Billy needed. With a quick jerk, he was free from the principal's grasp. In two jumps, his hand was on the doorknob, pulling the door open, just wide enough that he could slip through. The sound the door made as he slammed it shut behind himself didn't drown out the screaming cuss words the principal was spitting out as he came charging out the door in hot pursuit.

Fear seemed to put wings on Billy's heels as he flew down the hall, with those thundering footsteps close behind.

Going out the door at the end of the hall, Billy faked as if going down the step; instead he grabbed the handrail and vaulted over. He felt a big hand brush his shirt, followed by another string of curses.

Billy hit the ground running; the maneuver of jumping over the rail had picked up precious ground. By the time Billy reached the bridge, Mr. McPherson had gained back the lost ground and was stepping right on Billy's heels.

In another desperate move to put some distance between him and the principal, Billy pulled another fake, running full tilt as if he was going to cross the bridge. Billy, at the last possible second, darted to his right, around the corner of the bridge, jumping off the low embankment. He thought he might be going down, but in a few stumbling steps, he regained his stride. Mr. McPherson trying to duplicate Billy's move but, not being as nimble of feet, went crashing into the guardrail, which brought out a grunt of pain and another outpouring of cusses.

In the meantime, Billy had made it across the wash and up the far bank. Giving a quick look over his right shoulder, he could see

BILLY YOU, NO MORE HILLS

Mr. McPherson coming across the bridge in long running strides. He had stopped his cursing and screaming. There was a look of determination on his face as he was putting all his effort in trying to overtake Billy. Just ahead was the start of a long steep grade going up the side of the hill that the Adamses had built their home on; the house was sitting off to Billy's left.

As Billy's feet hit the base of the hill and started up it, a thrill of victory went through Billy. No one could catch him running up hill, he hoped.

The boys' home sat on a large piece of land. On the east end of the building, close by, was the younger boys' play area, with their swings, their slides, and other playing equipment. On past that was the older boys' play area, basketball court, tennis courts, and ball diamond. Beyond that was a fenced garden plot and a long chicken house. The boys grew most of the garden vegetables and kept laying hens that furnished them fresh eggs. On the west side of the building was a long, steep, slopping hill. All the grounds were fenced in with a high chain-link fence.

As far back as Billy could remember, he had liked to run, and on the long steep hill is where he did most of it. Like the steps out in front, this hill had become a challenge. At the age of five, he started out to conquer this hill. By the time he was nine, he had it conquered. He could sprint to the top, go back down, and sprint back to the top.

Every now and then, some boy or another would challenge Billy to a race up the hill. He loved it; not one boy in that home could out run him up that hill. Some of the older boys could best him to the base of the hill and for a short distance up it before he could pass them, and pass them he did, every time.

And now he was hoping and praying that all that uphill running he had done at the home would save him from those clutching hands that he could feel inches from his back. The principal gasped out, "Stop, you little bastard!" These words goaded him Billy into a faster pace, and now the rasping breath was falling further behind. Billy took another quick look over his shoulder. Mr. McPherson's mouth was wide open, struggling to get air into his lungs; his arms

CLARENCE W. LESLIE

were flopping about as if to propel him up the hill faster. Then as Billy watched, Mr. McPherson's legs seemed to turn to rubber. His arms began flagging around as if trying to propel himself forward, coming to a stop. Throwing his head back, he gasped for air. Billy became concerned. He moved down but maintained a safe distance from where the principal was on his knees, making terrible gasping sounds and clutching his chest. The principal's eyes glared at Billy. 'I'll get you for this."

"Sir, I'm sorry, I apologize for what I did."

"You're sorry—yes, you are a sorry little son of a bitch."

Billy flared up. "What about you and your crybaby son? You about beat me to death for something he started. Heck, all I did is pop him one little time on the nose and he went sniveling and crying to you."

The principal tried to struggle to his feet and failed. He screamed at Billy, "I'll get you, I'll get you." Billy knew that he meant it. That left him with only one thing to do: try and find his way back to the Mayhill Boys' Home.

He went up the hill at a trot until he was out of sight of the principal, then he ran full speed to the house. Running upstairs to his room, he jerked two quilts off his bed and rolled them up.

Heading back downstairs, he found a rope in the garage. Tying his so-called bedroll up, he made a sling where he could carry the rolled-up quilts across his back. Running back into the kitchen, he opened the refrigerator. Mrs. Adams always bought bologna and cheese in bulk so you could slice the meat or cheese the thickness you wanted. Billy cut a thick piece off each and found a plastic bag to put them in. Going back out into the garage, he took a glass jar with a handle on it from a shelf, where Mrs. Adams kept all kinds of jars and bottles stored. Going back into the kitchen, he rinsed the bottle out and filled it with water. He spied a salt shaker on the table and guessed he might need some salt before he got to where he was going. Opening up a drawer, he tore a small piece of tinfoil off a roll. Taking the top off the salt shaker, he put the piece of tinfoil over the top and screwed the lid back on; now he wouldn't lose his salt. He looked around, trying to think of something else he might need on

BILLY YOU, NO MORE HILLS

his long trip. Bread—he would need bread to go with his bologna and cheese. There was a half loaf in the bread box; he put that in the sack with the other food.

Now he was ready. Going back out into the garage, he hesitated; there was a large dirty window with junk piled in front of it. By standing on his tiptoes, he could look out of it and see the schoolhouse.

He was thankful that he had hesitated. There was a police car parked in the school yard with a policeman and Mr. McPherson standing beside it, looking his way, and Mr. McPherson was pointing at the house.

There was a front door going out of the living room. While Billy had lived here, he had never seen it open. Billy could go out that way without being seen from the school yard. The door had an old-fashioned key in the door lock, turning the key to the open position. Billy pulled on the door; it was stuck shut from not having been used in so long. He could hear the police car coming toward the house. Billy gave a frantic jerk then another; the door came open, with a squeaky protest. There was a screen door that came open easy.

Billy heard the police car pull up and stop in front of the garage. By the time the car doors slammed shut, he was going up the hill at a full run. By the time he had reached the shadow of the trees, he had winded himself. With hands on knees, trying to catch his breath, he heard the police car start up and leave the house. With his breath back, he moved on up the hill, climbing a short ways; the hill tapered out.

In front of Billy there was a wide clearing with a narrow two-rutted road running through it, and on the far side of the clear space, there were more trees. As Billy hesitated, pondering the thought of whether to cross that open ground, he again heard the sound of the police car. It hadn't come into view yet, but for sure it was coming down the dirt road that Billy was standing on the edge of. Darting back among the trees, he found a thick bushy bush to hide behind. Peeking through his cover, he watched the car go past. Mr. McPherson was riding with the policeman. They were both scanning the trees and bushes as they drove.

When they were out of sight and hearing, Billy moved from his hiding spot, and on flying feet, he raced across the open field and into the protection of the trees on the far side. After a brief wait, the car came back down the dirt road, still moving slowly.

After it was gone, Billy gave a sigh of relief and moved out on his long journey in his quest to find the Mayhill Boys' Home.

Chapter 6

He knew to go east, because when he had left with the Adamses they had driven due west. He started off at a fast jog then slowed to a walk. He had a long distance to travel; no need to wear himself out the first few miles.

When the sun was high in the sky, he stopped to rest a while and have a cheese-and-bologna sandwich.

Proceeding on his way, he felt somewhat rested, so he picked up his pace. He watched the sun swing to the west. He knew that sometime before dark, he was going to have to find a shelter for the night or sleep out in the open.

Then with the sun sinking fast, he came around a bend in the dirt road, and there up ahead, he could see a sand and gravel pit, with heavy equipment scattered about. Approaching with caution, he found the equipment to be old and dilapidated and the sand pit abandoned. Catching his eye was a rusty dump truck. With his eyes darting warily about, he approached the truck; all four tires were flat. Stepping up on the running board, he looked inside. It was a dusty, dirty mess, but it would be a good place to spend the night. Breaking a small branch off a tree, he dusted the seat off the best he could and spread his bedroll out.

With night coming fast, he made himself another sandwich and ate. Rolling his bedroll out on the truck seat and wrapping himself up in it, he hoped he would be able to sleep.

CLARENCE W. LESLIE

The warm sun shining through the cracked windshield woke Billy up. Raising himself up on one elbow, he rubbed his eyes, trying to clear the sleep away. It was long moments before Billy realized where he was.

Sitting straight up and looking wildly about, he expected to see the old truck surrounded by police cars with cops leaning over their car hoods with guns aimed at him. He breathed a sigh of relief; he was going to have to keep his imagination under control. There was not a thing out there but the same old rusty equipment that was there when he had gone to sleep.

But there was no need to get careless; someone could drive by any moment and find him sitting in the old truck, and there was no way to escape. In a hurry, Billy rolled up his sleeping bag and slung it across his back. Taking his food and water, he moved quickly away from the sand pit into the protection of the nearby trees. Feeling safe here, he took time to make himself a sandwich, washing it down with water. He was ready to move on.

The way he had it calculated in his head, one more night on the road and he would be back sleeping on his cot in the hallway in the safety of the Mayhill Boys' Home.

He kept walking east and angling to his right some as he went. He remembered crossing a river while riding with Mr. and Mrs. Adams. So somewhere on the way back, he had to cross that river. By drifting to the right as he traveled, he felt that eventually he would find the river and, hopefully, a bridge to cross over it on. The sun drifted higher and then was overhead. It was lunchtime. While fixing himself a sandwich, Billy observed that his food supply was getting mighty low. Oh well, sometime tomorrow he would be back at the boys' home with no worries.

As he trudged on, up ahead he could see dark clouds gathering and moving his way. He kept a wary eye on them. They kept getting closer and darker, and he could see lighting flashes dancing across them.

A breeze was kicking up, and he could feel moisture in it. He was going to have to find shelter and find it fast. He broke into a run,

BILLY YOU, NO MORE HILLS

moving straight into the fast-approaching deadly looking thunder heads.

As he was running along a ridge, out of the corner of his eye, he saw an old wooden windmill, and past the windmill stood a small wooden shed. He felt big cold raindrops begin to pound on his back as he went hurling off the ridge, trying to make it to the safety of the building before the storm hit him with its full force.

Billy wouldn't admit it to anyone, but he was terrified of lightning. Lightning flashes were all around him; it looked like great big snakes of fire dancing in the clouds.

The fear put wings to his heels as he flew toward the shelter of the little shed. As he began to think that he was going to make it, he saw a dog come out of the building through the open door, then another and another then one more. Billy broke stride; with heads down, the dogs were coming at him, and they were coming fast.

Three of the dogs were barking as they came. The dog leading the pack was huge, and he wasn't making a sound. With teeth bared, he was coming straight at Billy with one thought in mind.

Fear of the lightning was gone; it was replaced with a greater fear: the fear of what this massive beast would do if it got a hold of him and brought him down, and with the other dogs joining in, they would tear him to pieces.

The windmill was between them and him. He was closer to the tower than they were, but their speed was far greater than his; it was going to be close. Thank God the ladder going to the top of the windmill was facing him. If he could only reach it in time, he felt that it would save his life.

The three smaller dogs were coming around the side of the wooden base of the windmill, barking their heads off. The big one was coming straight underneath the base with teeth bared, still not making a sound. Billy made a desperate leap for the bottom rung of the ladder, at the same time reaching high for an upper rung. As he was flying through the air, he gave thanks for all the time he had practiced jumping up the front steps of the home.

The big brute came under the ladder at the same moment Billy's foot hit the bottom rung. The force of his foot hitting the old wooden rung shattered it. Billy's frantically grasping hands caught a secure hold on a rung overhead. He prayed that this one wouldn't break like the one his foot had broken. Desperately he jerked his feet up from the gaping jaws of the lunging dog. He felt the teeth close onto the heel of his left shoe; the weight of the dog came close to pulling him loose from his tight grip on the ladder. Billy began stomping down hard on the dog's nose and face with the heel of his right shoe. It worked; the dog let out a yelp of pain and gave up his hold on Billy's shoe.

Climbing up a few rungs, Billy looked down at the dogs. The big mean one was sitting on his haunches, looking up. The other three were fighting over something on the ground. Billy let out a moan of despair. The thing they were fighting over was his cheese, bologna, and bread. Another flash of lightning lit up the area. He could see his bottle of water lying there. He had lost everything in his desperate leap to safety.

The big cold raindrops were beginning to come down harder now. He started scrambling up the ladder. The only protection he was going to have from the storm was to get up as close as he could to the windmill decking. The storm was coming from the east. As he reached the bottom side of the decking, he found a cross timber. Easing out on that, he inched his way to the west side of the windmill, trying to get as far away from the driving rain as he possibly could.

Surprisingly, there was more protection from the storm than he had hoped for. In the next lightning flash, he could see the dogs, with heads down, dashing for the old shed, seeking protection of their own. The storm seemed to intensify as he huddled there on his precarious perch. After what seemed like an eternity to Billy, the storm began to recede, and then it was over.

There was no way he could get off the windmill and be safe from the threat of the dogs until daylight, so he could see what his options were to plan his escape and get back on his journey in search of the Mayhill Boys' Home.

He couldn't stay in this cramped position. He would be better off on top of the windmill deck, where he could stretch out and be

BILLY YOU, NO MORE HILLS

comfortable. With this thought in mind, he carefully inched his way back to the wooden ladder, then climbed up it to the deck.

There were millions of stars overhead and a big bright moon lighting up the world and the windmill deck, where he could see to spread out his bedroll in the safest location, not that there was a real safe place. The windmill was too high and the deck too small. But it would do.

Looking up at the sky, Billy said, "Thank you, God, for giving me the moon to see by." Then Billy thought he was being a little bit too generous with his thanks, so he added, "I'm assuming you did it for me."

Billy wrapped his bedroll around himself and lay down.

Billy was damp, the bedroll was damp, the wooden deck was damp, and Billy was cold. He lay there shivering, dozing fitfully off and on, until finally, out of exhaustion, he fell asleep. The sound of a car woke him. Startled, he woke up. A beat-up old pickup truck was pulling off the road and coming down toward the windmill.

In a panic Billy lay back down, squeezing himself as flat against the deck as possible, hoping that the driver of the truck wouldn't be able to see him. He had slept way too late; the sun was high in the sky. The warmth felt good after the chill of the night. Billy wasn't thinking about the warmth as he lay with his cheek pressed tight against the boards, hearing the truck bouncing and rattling, coming closer and closer to his hiding place on the deck of the high windmill. He let out a sigh of relief as the pickup bounced on by.

Casually he raised his head and peeked over the side. The old pickup came to a squeaking halt in front of a fence gate. An old country-type man got out of the pickup and walked to the gate. Billy flattened himself back against the boards that he was laying on. Another vehicle was coming down off the road. As it moved past the windmill, Billy raised his head enough to look over the side. He felt his heart skip a beat.

It was a police car. A young cop got out of it as the old cowboy strolled back his way.

"Good morning, Officer, you're a mite off your beaten path, aren't you?"

"Morning, Ed. I'm looking for a runaway. You haven't seen a young fellow wandering around this part of the country, have you?"

The old man took his hat off and scratched his balding head.

"No, I sure haven't—course I haven't been up here in the last three or four days. Who does he belong to?"

"He doesn't belong to anyone. He's an orphan boy, been staying with the Adamses, back down the road in town."

The old man scratched his head again. "Don't know the folks. Why did he run away?"

"I don't really know why! But according to the principal at the school, he's a bad kid. 'Nothing but trouble from the first day he started school there." Billy came close to jumping up and shouting "That's a lie!" but restrained himself with great effort.

The old cowboy pointed at the shed. "Might be a good idea to have a look inside that building there. The runaway could have stayed the night in there, could possibly still be in there." The police officer, moving toward the building, said, "I'll have a look-see."

The old cowboy called after him. "Be careful, there have been reports of wild dogs around here. A neighbor claims they're a mite vicious."

The officer, upon reaching the doorway, pulled the gun out of his holster on his hip and cautiously stepped inside the rundown old building. After a short period, he came back out; his gun was back in his holster. "Nope—no boy, no dogs. I'll go on down the road a ways if we don't find him. I expect when he gets hungry he'll come back. Take care of yourself, Ed."

"You too, Officer." Billy stayed on top of the windmill until the sound of both vehicles had faded away.

He was starved; he hadn't had anything to eat since noon yesterday, and now it was the middle of the morning, and the dogs had gobbled up the last of his food the night before, and he had no clue where his next meal would come from. Well, at least the dogs were gone; he didn't have to worry about them. He decided that he should leave this area before the dogs decided to come back. Scrambling down the ladder, he retrieved his water bottle from where it had bounced against a leg of the windmill. Unscrewing the cap, he took a big swig. It wasn't food, but it helped. Heaving a big sigh, Billy headed east once more.

Hopefully, by the end of the day, he would have reached the Mayhill Boys' Home or be close enough to where it would be but a short walk the next day. Back on the dirt road, he moved out at a fast trot. Shortly the road swung in a southerly direction. Coming over a rise, Billy stopped. Sitting down below him was a neat-looking little town with a wide-paved road going through it.

Billy didn't remember passing through this town while traveling with the Adamses. But it could have been while he was asleep before Mrs. Adams had awoken him up with her loud snoring. Billy wished that he dared to go into town and look for something to eat, but he knew that would be a foolish thing to do. He would be picked up and hauled back to Mr. McPherson's office, and that thought sent a shiver of fear shooting through his body. He wouldn't get foolish and let that happen. The paved road ran east and west; that lifted Billy's spirits, with the thought that he had probably been traveling in the right direction.

He now left the dirt road that he had been following and began to skirt his way around the town. There was plenty of scrub pinion and cedar to conceal himself from the view of anyone who just might be looking up this way.

The houses began to spread out, getting farther and farther apart. The high ground that Billy was on began to level out, and the scrub trees were suddenly gone. A short distance in front of him was a small white house with blue trim.

Billy decided right then and there that this was the place that he would try to get something to eat at. Hiding his bedroll and water bottle in some tall weeds, he approached the house. He had no clue to what he would say to the person that would answer the door; he would just have to play it by ear.

The house had a low white picket fence around it, and as Billy went in through the gate, he couldn't help but notice that the small lawn was in bad need of a mowing. That was his opening; he would offer to mow their lawn for a sandwich or whatever.

Walking up to the door, Billy heaved a big sigh and rapped on it. There was no answer. He rapped again—still no answer. Maybe the folks were out in back some place and couldn't hear his knock. Moving around to the back of the house, Billy found a screened-in back porch. He gave a sharp rap on the screen door—still no answer.

He pulled on the door handle; the door wasn't locked. Sticking his head in, he hollered, "Anyone home?" No response. Billy let his eyes move over the room. The two pies seemed to jump right out at him. They were sitting on a counter in covered dishes, Billy tiptoed over and lifted the lid of each one and smelled; they were both apple.

It took all his control to keep from digging both hands in and to start eating, but he held back. First he had to earn it. He remembered the tall lawn grass. Going back outside, he spied a small shed. Sure enough, inside the shed was a push lawn mower.

Billy had mowed the grass at the boys' home many times with a mower similar to this one. In no time the lawn was mowed and the lawn mower back in the shed.

In his heart, Billy didn't know if he was doing the right thing to cut into one of those pies and eat a piece of it, but he was hungry and he had done some work. He felt that justified him eating some pie. Going back inside the screened porch, he looked around but couldn't find a knife to cut the pie with. There was a door going from the porch into the house.

Opening this door, Billy found himself looking into the kitchen. Once more, to make sure no one was inside, he let out a loud "Hello!" No answer. In the second drawer he opened, he found a knife and fork, in one of the cupboards a plate. He cut the pie in half, then cut one of the halves in half. One of the quarters is what he ate; it was delicious. Billy eyed the other quarter but felt that he had not done enough work to eat any more of the pie. There was a solution to that. Quickly going back outside, he found a rake and a wheelbarrow in the same shed that he had found the mower. In a few minutes of fast raking, he had the grass raked and piled into the wheelbarrow.

Now feeling that he had earned that other piece of pie, Billy gobbled it down, relishing every bite. It was just as delicious as the

BILLY YOU, NO MORE HILLS

first piece. This made him think of Mr. Cook's pies; no one's pies could match the ones that that tough old man baked.

Billy could hear Mr. Cook saying, "A dab more shortening in the crust is all it takes." Billy didn't know exactly how much a dab was, but now there was something he could do to help pay for the pie he had eaten. Back in the kitchen he found a notepad and pencil and wrote out a message for the pie maker.

> Dear ma'am,
>
> I was real, real hungry, so I ate half of one of your pies. I did some work in your yard to help pay for it. The pie was real good.
>
> Thanks,
> Billy
>
> PS: Put a dab more shortening in your crust.

Billy had heard—or thought he had heard—if you had something important to say, you should put a *PS* in front of it.

Billy had given a little thought about signing his name—should he or shouldn't he? He had been stepping over the line a bit lately—it was time to stop, so he signed his name.

Now sensing a need to hurry, he moved out, closing the door and gate behind him. Billy sprinted back to where his belongings were.

The sound of a car coming sent a wave of fear flowing through him. Scooping up his bedroll and water bottle, on the run, Billy darted into some tall weeds. Diving into them headfirst, his flattened body hugged the ground.

The car came to a stop in front of the house Billy had just vacated. Cautiously he raised his head and peeked through the weeds.

An old couple got out and went into the house. As the door closed behind them, Billy was up and running. He mentally patted himself on the back for telling the lady about the shortening that would help pay for the pie.

Chapter 7

There wasn't much cover, so he hugged the low spots as much as possible. Upon reaching what he felt to be a safe distance from the highway, Billy once more headed east following the road.

In a short while, the small town and scattered buildings were far behind him. With a full stomach, Billy's spirits had lifted.

Hopefully before nightfall, he would be back at the Mayhill Boys' Home. But his hopes began to fade as the sun climbed up and over him and began to fall rapidly into the west. The pie was wearing off, and his water supply was getting low. It was beginning to look like he would be spending another night sleeping out in the open and, to make it worse, without food.

As Billy was despondently jogging along, he began picking up a sound, a rumbling sound. It took him a while to realize what it was, but finally it dawned on him: it was a train. Something else dawned on him: he couldn't recall seeing a train or a railroad tracks on his trip with the Adamses. A little bit of doubt began to seep in that maybe, just maybe, he wasn't traveling in the right direction to find the boys' home.

Now he could see the train; it was coming in from his left. The tracks the train were on made a long sweeping curve. Up ahead, the tracks straightened out and ran parallel to the highway. Moving ahead, Billy reached the point where the road and tracks ran side by side. If he stayed between the two, he would be far too close to the

BILLY YOU, NO MORE HILLS

highway and could be easily seen. He waved at the train crew as the train went thundering past.

Then crossing over the tracks, he was hidden from view from the occasional vehicles using the highway.

The sun was sinking fast into the west, and Billy's hopes were sinking just as fast, with the knowledge that he wasn't going to reach the boys' home on this day. His goal now was to find some type of shelter to spend the night in or under.

Then as dusk was setting in, he saw a flicker of light up ahead. He quickened his already fast pace; he could make out that it was a campfire. Drawing closer yet, he could hear voices. Now he could make out two silhouettes sitting by the fire—two men. He eased up another few feet. At times they seemed to be arguing, then they would burst into laughter. He was close enough now to see that the men were passing a bottle back and forth and taking swigs out of it.

An odor came drifting out to Billy, an odor of food. He hadn't realized how hungry he was until the smell of that food reached him. He called out.

"Hello, the fire!"

One of the men jumped up. "What the hell! Who is out there?"

The cussing made Billy think of Mr. Cook—not that Mr. Cook cursed, but by the fact that he didn't cuss. The cook was one rough, tough old man, but Billy had never heard him utter a cuss word.

Now it seemed, since he had been away from the home, that most of the people cussed—oh, well! He stepped into the circle of the campfire light.

"My name is Billy, I just happened to be passing by. I saw your fire and smelled your food. I wonder if you would mind sharing some of it with me?"

"Hear that, Josh, some kid wants to eat the rest of our stew?"

Now the other man spoke up. "Move over here, boy, so we can get a better look at you."

Billy did as he was told. The man that had spoke up first was a short, heavy-looking guy with a big round, shiny bald head. The other was a tall gaunt man with grey, shaggy, thinning hair.

Billy was surprised; they both looked fairly neat and clean.

CLARENCE W. LESLIE

The tall one stepped up close to Billy. "Are you running away from home, boy?"

"No, sir, I'm on my way back home."

This brought a couple of gruff laughs out of the men.

"How old are you, boy?"

"Twelve, sir."

"What about it, Josh, do you think a twelve-year-old should be leaving his paw and ma?"

"Nope, I don't think any kid should run away from home before the age of fourteen."

That brought some more gruff laughter out of the two. Billy didn't care how much they laughed and made fun of the situation; he sure wanted that stew. Out of the corner of his eye, he spotted a can lying away from the fire. So it was canned stew; it still smelled awful good.

Maybe if he made himself sound humble and polite, he would get better results out of these two clowns.

"Please, sir." He put a little whine in his voice. "Just a few bites of your food, then I'll go and leave you alone."

The heavy man reached out and grabbed Billy by the arm. In one quick motion, he spun Billy around and stripped his bedroll over his head and off. Billy let out a yell, "What the heck do you think you're doing?" That brought a vicious shove from the man, sending Billy sprawling flat.

There was fright in Billy's voice as he let out a yelp. "Hey!"

As he was trying to scramble to his feet, the same man delivered a swift kick to the seat of his pants; that kick hurt.

Billy came up running, with jeering laughter following him. At a safe distance, he stopped and shouted back at the two. "Hey! It's going to get cold out here tonight. I need my bedroll."

"Boy, if you don't get the hell out of here, I'm going to give you more of what you just got. Now get on home. I'm keeping this blanket you call a bedroll, it's going to help keep me warm this coming winter." That brought more laughs from the two.

Billy slunk out into the darkness a ways and sat down behind a bush. The last mile or so, the shrubbery had begun to thicken up

BILLY YOU, NO MORE HILLS

again. What the heck was he going to do? The air was rapidly cooling off; he needed his bedroll. Scooting around to the side of the bush, he sat where he could keep his eye on the camp. The two were passing the bottle back and forth between them again.

The fire seemed to be dying down, and they hadn't added any wood to it for a while.

He could hear them talking but was too far away to hear what they were saying. After what seemed like forever, with the night getting cooler by the minute and the fire getting dimmer, one of the men, the tall one, stood up and stretched. He then walked out into the night, away from the fire. Going out to relieve himself, Billy felt. Upon returning, he sat down on his bedroll and began removing his shoes. The dumpy man had already taken his shoes off and was crawling into his bed.

The fire was barely flickering as the tall man slid under his covers. Billy moved to within a few feet from where the two hobos were lying. Hobos were what Billy had determined these two were.

He had never met a hobo but had heard about them and had read some about them. In a short while, one of the men began to snore; in a minute or two, the other joined in. Inching his way over to where the man that had stolen Billy's bedroll was sleeping, Billy could see a corner of it sticking out from underneath the mess that fat boy was sleeping on.

Billy was relieved to see that the man's big round dirty head was not sleeping on it. Moving to the fire, he took a lid off of a smoked-up pot. Sitting close by, the smell of that stew came wafting up to him. Those two pieces of pie were long gone, and Billy was starved. Sticking his finger in the pot, then into his mouth, he tasted it. He was so hungry Billy thought it tasted better than any food that he had ever eaten. He racked up the coals in the fire and added a few twigs, all the while keeping the corner of his eyes on the two snoring and sleeping men. He placed the stew pan on the fire, then while he was waiting for it to heat up, he tiptoed around the campsite.

Over by the tall one's bed, he found the bottle that the two men had been drinking out of. It was a gallon wine bottle, still about a third full. Chuckling to himself, Billy poured the wine out.

Nosing around further, he came across two gallon bottles with water in them. One was full; the other had about the same amount of water to match the wine that he had poured out. He poured the part of a bottle of water into the wine bottle and sat it back where he had found it.

Testing the stew, he found it ready. He looked around. He needed a spoon or fork—something to eat with. Lying by the empty stew can was a small canvas bag. Inside he found an assortment of mismatched utensils. Picking out a spoon, he burned the spoon part in the hot coals for a moment. He felt that if these two had any bad germs, the heat would kill them. After the spoon had cooled off enough, he dug into the stew. It was as delicious as it smelled. He ate until he was pleasantly stuffed.

Then retrieving the empty stew can, he rinsed it thoroughly clean and put the remaining stew in it. With a little bit of looking around, he found his water bottle he had dropped when he had been shoved and kicked. He placed the spoon in the can of stew then took the can and his water bottle out away from the camp and hid them behind a bush. Now he was ready to reclaim his bedroll. The hobos had gathered up a large supply of firewood. Billy stacked it all on the bed of coals.

While he was waiting for it to catch fire and burn big, he spied the two men's shoes sitting beside their respective bedrolls. He took both pairs and tied their four shoelaces together in hard knots. He then scooped up dirt with his hands and filled each shoe with it, then he took what was left of their water and poured that into their shoes also.

Taking their shoes out away from the camp, he hid them behind another bush. With all his activity, neither man had moved or stopped snoring.

By now the fire was really taking hold. It was lighting up the whole surrounding area. It was time for action.

Billy went and kneeled by the top of the bald-headed man's head. The fire was blazing real high; he could feel the heat away over here. With a firm grip on the corner of his blanket, he leaned over and yelled into the man's ear, "Fire! Fire!" The man grunted and missed a snore or two but didn't move. Billy felt around on the ground and came up with a round rock about the size of a chicken egg. He raised it up and let out a piercing scream, "Fire!" and, at the same moment, gave the man a sharp rap on the forehead with the rock. That brought galvanized action.

The heavy man jumped straight up out of his bedroll, and he was screaming, "Fire! Fire!" at the top of his lungs. That brought the skinny man to life; he came jumping out of his bedroll and, in the process, got his legs tangled up and fell flat on his face. The scream he let out was a scream of fear. He must have thought the world was coming to an end or something terrible was attacking them.

By now Billy was laughing so hard he could hardly pull his blanket from beneath the bedroll. They were jumping up and down and yelling; they hadn't seen him. He backed out of the circle of fire-light and stood in the darkness, watching and listening to the show they were putting on.

"What in the hell possessed you to pile all that wood on the fire?"

"Me! What do you mean me?"

"It had to be you—heck, I was sound asleep!"

"If you didn't do it and I didn't do it, who did?"

The tall one yelled at the short one, "Claude, you drank so damn much of that wine you probably put the wood on there and don't remember it."

"Me? Me? Why you drank as much as I did. I swear every time you tilted that bottle up, your old Adam's apple would jump up and down with two or three swallows!"

The one called Josh started to protest, but Claude cut him short.

"Speaking about wine, pass me that bottle." The tall one did as he was instructed. Claude uncapped it and took a long swig and smacked his lips before he realized that he wasn't drinking wine. He let out a bellow.

"Damn you, Josh, I said wine not water." Josh charged Claude, bellowing right back, "Don't you cuss and yell at me—by god, I won't stand for it. Look at the label on the bottle, you stupid fool, and see what it says."

Billy was rocking with laughter as the two stood screaming and cussing each other. In the middle of a screaming sentence, Baldy stopped and said, "That kid, that blasted kid!"

Billy stepped back into the circle of light.

"That blasted kid is right here."

Both men whirled on him. But before either one could say anything, Billy shook a corner of his blanket. "I came back and got my bedroll. And by the way, you guys are really good cooks, the stew was fabulous."

Claude let out a string of curses and charged Billy. On his first step, he let out a yell of pain and grabbed his foot. Then, while hopping around on one foot, he stepped on another sharp object, which brought out more yelps of pain. He flopped down on his bedroll and, pointing at Josh, barked out, "Hand me my shoes."

Turning to Billy with his finger still pointing, he said, "Kid, you're going to rue the day you crossed old Claude here."

"Josh, where the hell are my shoes?" Josh had been gingerly tiptoeing around so as not to end up with bruised feet like his partner.

"Claude," he said in a puzzled voice, "your shoes are gone. So are mine." Claude's mouth fell open as he began to sputter, but no words came out.

Billy spoke up. "Gentlemen, our little get-together has been pleasant, but now it's time for me to move on. My advice to you is go back to bed and get a good night's sleep, and in the morning sunlight, I'm sure you'll find your shoes. 'Night! Night!"

With that, he turned and disappeared into the darkness, chuckling to himself. He looked up. "Pretty neat the way I handled that, don't you think?" Then he added, "You don't have to answer. I just want you to know that I'm doing a good job of taking care of myself."

Now he had to find a safe place to sleep. There were lots of stars out, but it was still very dark, so he had to feel his way along, as he needed to put as much distance between himself and the two hobos as he could. He didn't think that they would come looking for him come daylight, but you could never tell what two guys like those might do.

BILLY YOU, NO MORE HILLS

The edge of a big moon began to come up, and it seemed with every step he took, it got bigger and higher. Now he was back into the small trees and bushes. He needed to find a place where he would be concealed from the pair if they came stumbling along this way.

The moon was out big and bright; now Billy could see where he was going. Up ahead and off to the right a ways, he could see what appeared to be a thick stand of bushes. Moving over to them, he eased his way through the heavy growth. At one point, the branches became so dense that he had to force his way past them.

Suddenly he was in a small moonlit clearing, a perfect place to spend the night. Spreading out his bedroll, he lay down, but sleep wouldn't come.

There seemed to be little noises all around. He could imagine bears or mountain lions creeping up on him. Or maybe Claude and Josh had trailed him here and, at this very moment, were ready to pounce on him.

At every small sound, he would jerk upright, looking wildly around, until out of sheer exhaustion, he fell sound asleep.

Chapter 8

The hot, bright sun shining in his eyes woke Billy up.

He came scrambling out of his bed in a panic. The sun was high in the sky; he had slept far later than he intended to. Quickly rolling up his bed and slinging it over his shoulder, he was ready to face a new day and whatever it brought with it. The stew can was sitting where he had placed it last night. He would have liked to take it with him and eat it later in the day because this would probably be the only food he would have this day. But his good sense told him that he had better eat it now.

Food like this sitting in an open can might spoil, and he sure didn't want to come down with food poisoning.

The stew was cold and didn't taste as good as it had the night before. But Billy knew that it would give him strength to get through the day, and he hoped with all his might that by the time the evening meal came around, he would be sitting in the mess hall eating Mr. Cook's cooking.

Moving out of his hiding place, he casually looked around. He could see nothing to be alarmed over, so he moved out at a fast pace. He was getting a very late start, and he wanted to make up as much time as possible. As fast as he was moving, the sun seemed to be moving faster. It reached its overhead peak and was sliding fast down behind him. As the afternoon was waning, clouds began climbing up from the east, and a cool breeze seemed to come out of nowhere. So far, he had not seen a house or any other sign of inhabitants.

BILLY YOU, NO MORE HILLS

He had a weird feeling that he might be the only one left on earth. The black clouds were coming toward Billy as fast as the sun was falling behind him, and now he could feel a fine moisture in the air.

He hadn't covered much ground today, and it didn't look like he was going to go much farther; he needed to find some shelter and find it fast.

His big disappointment was that he was going to have to spend another night away from the home and not go to bed full of one of Mr. Cook's delicious meals.

Darkness was just about upon him, but in the distance, he could see a few scattered lights.

Hopefully somewhere among those lights, he might find an old barn or shed of some kind that he could slip into and be out of the weather. The houses were scattered—mostly mobile homes—and they all had fences around them. It was dark enough now that it would be hard to be seen by anyone as he prowled around through the neighborhood.

The houses thinned out, and there was still no shelter.

He was about to give up hope when he stumbled into a wooden fence. He immediately noticed that the cold wind wasn't hitting him here. Leaning back against the fence, he slid down to a sitting position. It wasn't much, but it would have to do. The stew that he had eaten for breakfast was long gone, and now he found the prospect of a long, probably cold night.

He was more tired than he realized; he had no more stretched out than he was sound asleep.

He was back on his cot in the hallway, sleeping peacefully and enjoying it very much, then for no reason Billy could understand, Mr. Cook, the cook, came in and began to kick him in the side.

Billy, trying to scoot back away from the kick, yelling, "Stop it! Stop it!" This brought a harder kick, jarring Billy awake. Startled, he jumped up, looking wildly around. There was one of the biggest men he had ever seen standing in front of him and looking down at Billy.

"What the damned hell are you doing here, boy?"

Here was another person cussing at him. He wished that Mrs. Jamison could have all these foul-mouthed people under her thumb for a few days. They would be glad to clean up their act.

The man bent and, placing his hand on Billy's shoulder, shoved him back against the fence. "I asked you what the hell are you doing here on my property?"

There was a real bad odor, and it didn't take Billy long to realize that it was coming from this giant of a man. Billy looked him over. His huge head had long thinning straggly looking, dirty hair. All he appeared to have on was a baggie pair of bibbed coveralls, and as big as he was, the coveralls were too large for him. His heavy, dirty-looking bare arms were huge. On his feet he had a pair of low-cut run-down shoes, minus the shoelaces. The baggy coveralls liked six inches or so reaching the top of his shoes, his bare ankles were caked with what Billy thought of as crud.

"Talk to me, boy!"

Billy put a whine into his voice; he was getting good at this. "Please, sir, I meant no harm. I'm a long way from home, and when darkness caught up with me, I lay down along the side of your fence to get some protection from the wind and the cold." He couldn't tell if his whimpering and scheming was having any kind of effect on this odd-appearing man. So he threw some more on. "Please sir, if you will just turn loose of me, I'll be on my way."

Still holding on to Billy's arm, the foul-smelling man stooped over where he was, right in Billy's face.

"This is private property, boy. I've got a good mind to call the law on you." Billy thought the man's body odor was bad, but when he bent over and hit Billy with his breath, it about knocked him over. Twisting his head around and leaning back as far as he could, he pleaded one more time. "If you will turn me loose, sir, I'll leave and never come back! That's a promise, sir, and I'm a boy that never breaks his promise."

He threw that last part in just for good measure, but none of his pleading, whinnying, nor begging had any effect on this huge man. Still holding Billy's arm and jerking him along with him, he growled, "I'll take you to my wife, she'll know what to do."

Coming to a gate, the man lifted a latch, and the gate swung open. Shoving Billy through it, he closed the gate then hooked a padlock in a hasp, locking them on the inside. Billy looked around. It was big on the inside, with trash and junk scattered everywhere, and the whole place was fenced in with this high wooden fence that was higher than his head. The tall man let out a bellow: "Martha, get out here." Then before this person could possibly have time to react, he let out another bellow: "Martha!"

Then from a small square house Billy stood facing came a high, squeaky voice, "I'm coming, sweetie, I'm coming."

A huge round lady came out of an open door in that square house. It shocked Billy; he had been expecting to see a small woman to go along with that little voice. She had on a straight plain light-blue dress that came down way short of her knees. Her bare legs were bigger around than Billy's body. She came striding over to her husband, never looking at Billy.

"Yes, Delbert dear, what's wrong?"

Delbert pointed. "Look what I found."

She looked down at Billy as if this was the first time she had seen him standing there. She sounded surprised.

"Oh! It's a boy. Where did you find him, Delbert dear?"

Delbert pointed over his shoulder. "Trespassing!"

She looked at Billy with big round questioning eyes. "Is that right?"

Billy hoped that maybe he could get a little sympathy and understanding from this huge lady; her appearance was just the opposite of her husband's. Her dress looked fresh and clean. Her short blond hair was well groomed and shiny, and her face looked as if she had just applied her makeup. She had a sweet smile on her face as she waited for Billy to answer.

"Yes, ma'am, but it was dark, and I didn't know that I was trespassing."

She said "oh" and looked at her husband. *Good*, Billy thought, *she is going to give the big boy heck for treating me this way.*

"Martha, this boy was sleeping alongside our fence out there. What do you think we should do about it?"

She looked back at Billy, shaking her head from side to side. This dashed Billy's hopes.

"Well, Delbert dear. We're going to charge this young man a night's lodging, that's what we're going to do."

Billy let out a squawk of protest. "You want to make me pay for sleeping on your cold old ground?"

She gently took hold of Billy's shoulders. "That cold old ground is private property, and it's *our* private property, and that means that you owe us one night's rent."

He started to let out another protest, but she stopped him.

"No, no, now what's fair is fair." So saying, she placed a hand on one of her round piggy cheeks as if in thought. After a moment, she said, "Motels charge somewhere between forty and fifty dollars a night for one of their rooms." Looking at Billy, she said, "Isn't that right?"

"Ma'am, I wasn't in a motel room. I slept on your old hard ground."

She shook her finger at him. "Now, now, I didn't say I was going to charge you that much. Why, fifty or even forty dollars would be way too much. Delbert dear, what do you think we should charge this young man for a night's lodging?"

Delbert spread his hands wide. "Whatever you say, Martha, is good with me."

There was no doubt in Billy's mind who the boss was in this family. Once more placing a hand on her cheek, she stood there tapping a foot, in deep thought as she pondered the situation. Clapping her hands together, she smiled at Billy. "Thirty dollars, that's what I'll charge you, I asked you to be fair with me, and it's only right that I be fair with you." Holding out her hands, as if she expected him to plop thirty dollars into it, she asked, "Well?"

She had a big smile on her face showing two rows of gleaming white teeth. It entered his head that this lady must brush her teeth three or four times a day to keep them so nice and white, then it entered his head why was he standing here thinking about white teeth while this big smiling woman was holding out her open hand expecting him to plop thirty dollars into it, which didn't make any

BILLY YOU, NO MORE HILLS

sense to Billy. Something else that didn't make any sense to Billy was why a neat, clean lady like this would be married to a slob like Delbert. He didn't mean to shout again but he did. "Thirty dollars? Ma'am, I don't have thirty dollars. I don't have thirty cents. I don't have one penny to my name." Her eyes grew wide, and she began slowly shaking her head from side to side.

As she opened her mouth to speak, Billy beat her to it. "Ma'am, being as I don't have any money, I'll be on my way." So saying, he took a step toward the closed gate, hoping but not believing that they would let him leave.

It didn't happen; she took hold of his arm and pulled him back. "Not so fast, my young friend. Delbert, you heard him say that he didn't have the money to pay. What do you suppose we can do about that?"

Delbert's answer was a spreading of his hands and a shrug of his shoulders. Martha went into deep thought again, with head tilted back and eyes rolled upward, her hands clasped as if in prayer. Her face was contorted in a way that Billy thought she might be in terrible pain. Then giving a little squeal, she jumped up and clapped her hands together. Billy guessed it to be a jump. Her knees bent down and sprang up, but her feet never left the ground. "Chores," she chortled. "Delbert, we'll let the boy pay for his night's lodging by doing some chores around the place." She clapped her hands together in delight that she had come up with such a brilliant idea. Every thought she had seemed to be followed by a hand clap. To Billy it seemed as if she tried to do her little jump, but her body hadn't responded. "Delbert, dear, what do you think we should have this boy do?" Before Delbert could answer, she spoke to Billy. "Oh, I'm sorry I keep calling you Boy, how rude of me. What's your name, sweetie?"

Billy flinched at being called *sweetie*. "My name is Billy, ma'am." Before he could get out of the way, her big soft arms went around him and pulled him into her ample bosom in a long, hard squeeze. "Billy—what a wonderful boy's name that is." She threw her arms wide, and Billy staggered back, gasping for air. This woman's body was so soft it the felt like he had been engulfed in it.

72

"Delbert." She was still waiting for his answer.

"Whatever you want, Martha."

Placing her hands on her hips, Martha twisted to the right. Billy couldn't believe his eyes; her feet never moved, but that huge lady turned halfway around to where she could see behind herself, then that body slowly swung back around in that same wide arc. All the while, her eyes were scanning that big yard full of junk. Coming back around until she was once more facing Billy, she looked over his head, and her eyes lit up with a discovery, which brought another hard clap. Grabbing Billy by the shoulders, she spun him around so that he could see what she was seeing. It was a long, low building with screened sides halfway down on the near wall; the rest of the building was made from lumber.

"That's our chicken house." Jerking him around to the left, she said, "See that thing lying on its side—that's a wheelbarrow." The way she said it was as if he didn't know what a wheelbarrow was. "And see leaning over there against a post, that's a shovel. Now what we want you to do is clean out the chicken house." Her finger was pointing again. "Past the far end of the chicken house, there's an open spot—do you see it?"

"Yes, ma'am."

"That's where we want you to dump the chicken manure you clean out of the chicken house."

"OK." Billy let out another resigned "Yes, ma'am." As Billy angrily went to get the wheelbarrow and shovel, he looked up. "What makes me think that you and this mammoth woman are in on this together? You know I never ask you to help too much. All I'm asking is don't work against me." Still mumbling to himself, Billy began the task of cleaning out the chicken house. It was a mess inside; it looked like it hadn't been cleaned in years. As he was shoveling, he heard big Martha's high, squeaky voice calling to big Delbert.

"Delbert dear, have you fed the pigs yet?"

He answered, "No, Martha."

"Come, come, sweetie, let's get with it."

"Yes, Martha."

BILLY YOU, NO MORE HILLS

Billy shook his head; she sure pushed that big guy around. As Billy was starting on his second wheelbarrow load, a chicken began cackling, down at the far end of the coop. He knew what that meant. Usually when a hen lay an egg, she would let out a cackling sound. He supposed she was proudly announcing the arrival of the egg.

Looking to where the sound was coming from, Billy saw a big white chicken hop out of a laying nest and come strutting past him and out the door. He had been so angry when he came inside here to start cleaning the place out he had failed to look around. Now he could see that where the hen came from, there were two rows of laying nests, three nests to each row. In one of the top nests, another white chicken was sitting. Billy backed away; he didn't want to disturb her. As he was dumping his next load of chicken mess, the remaining hen on the nest began her proud cackling. As Billy was moving back, this hen, coming out the door, did her proud strut.

Back inside, he quickly moved down and peered into the nest. Each of the three top nests had two eggs in each in them. Billy had to have them; somehow he had to devise a plan to take the eggs with him when big Martha let him go.

Billy had begun his cleanup job in the doorway and had worked his way across to the far wall. As he was shoveling, his shovel point hit one of the wall boards. To his surprise, the board moved out a ways, and he could see daylight on the outside. Excited, he pushed the board open far enough to where he could stoop over and look out. The fence that Billy had slept against last night was used for this wall of the chicken house.

His spirits soared; he had found his escape route. At that moment, Delbert began shouting, "Martha, Martha, come quick."

Billy thought that he had been discovered pushing the wall out.

"The pigs got out, Martha, I need help."

Billy slipped over to the door and peeked out. Martha came charging out of the house and in her high-pitched voice answered her husband, "I'm coming, sweetie, Martha is coming to help." Billy had to laugh; the big lady was going to the rescue. She was bent forward at the waist. Her arms were pumping furiously back and forth, and her dainty feet, for such a large person, were pounding up and down, but she was making very little progress. To Billy it looked like a big bowl of Jell-O trying to run. Finally she disappeared through the piles of trash and junk, going toward the sound of Delbert's voice.

Billy's opportunity had come. He would grab the eggs and run. Over by a pile of trash, he spied a small bucket with a bail on it. It would be perfect. He could use it to carry the eggs in, then when he felt that he was a safe enough distance from the odd team of man and wife, he would build a campfire and have some hard-boiled eggs. The last meal that he had eaten was the last of the Hobo's stew yesterday morning. Getting the bucket, he gathered the eggs, then pushing the board aside, he wedged himself through the opening. His bedroll was down the fence a ways, still spread out on the ground, the way he had left it when big Delbert had woke him with his kicks and dragged him inside. Billy thought of it as their fort or compound.

Rolling up his bedroll so he could put it on in a hurry, he placed it beside the egg bucket and his water jar.

He could have grabbed his belongings and just disappeared, but he wouldn't have felt good about himself if he did it that way. He had to somehow get a small token of revenge. Going back through the fence, he could hear the pair still chasing the pigs.

Delbert was bellowing, the pigs were squealing, and Martha was squeaking.

The wheelbarrow was full of chicken manure; the door to the square house was wide open. It was get-even time. Grabbing the wheelbarrow by the handles, he sprinted across the yard with it and bounced it through the door. He was in the kitchen. In here it wasn't as bad as their messed-up yard, but was still cluttered up pretty good. Upending the wheelbarrow, he dumped the manure in the middle of the kitchen floor. Back to the chicken pen he went and loaded up again. This load went to the same place. Billy was getting a little nervous; he hoped he wasn't drawing it to fine. If Martha came through that door right now, he would be finished. He glanced hurriedly around. The kitchen table, besides being littered with pots, pans, and dishes, had three or four dozen fold-up matchbooks scattered around on it. Billy grabbed three of them and stuffed them in his pocket. Now he had a way to light his fire to cook his eggs on.

BILLY YOU, NO MORE HILLS

Pushing the wheelbarrow back out and into the chicken coop, he waited. He didn't have to wait long; Big Martha came striding back past the piled-up junk and trash. Her walk was twice as fast as her full-out sprint had been.

As she went into the house, Billy held his breath. It seemed to take forever; he began to think that that she had never even noticed it. He very nearly jumped out of his skin as a high, piercing scream came out of the house; it was more than Billy had expected. Martha's body filled the doorway, and she let out another scream.

"Delbert! Get your ass over here—right now!"

Billy wondered what had happened to the sweet names she had been calling her husband. Like *dearest* and *sweetie.*

Delbert came in a hurry, dragging his feet on the ground to keep his shoes from coming off.

Billy had to chuckle; no way this big man was going to catch him. Martha stepped aside, pointed, and said, "Look what that boy did to my house."

Delbert stepped inside, saying, "What did he do, Martha?"

"You fool, are you so blind you can't see that pile of chicken shit on my kitchen floor?"

Billy thought it wouldn't be wise for Mrs. Jameson to try and wash this big woman's mouth out. He could hear Delbert muttering something inside the house. His wife cut him off. "Go get that Billy boy and fetch him for me."

Billy felt sorry for poor Delbert. She was talking to him like he was a dog, telling him to go fetch something.

Billy stepped out of the chicken coop doorway, which made the big lady screech. "There he is."

Billy raised his hand and waved at her. "Good-bye, Martha." Before she could stop herself, a big smile lit up her face, and she waved back.

This brought another screech out of her, a screech of rage. "Fetch him." Delbert was getting close; it was time to go. He waved at the big man.

"Good-bye, Delbert, it was nice of you to let me clean your filthy chicken pen."

Delbert's response was a low growl.

Billy darted across the room and eased himself into the opening, ready to flee. Delbert let out a bellow of triumph.

"I've got him, Martha, he's trapped in the chicken pen." As he came charging through the door, he stopped dead in his tracks, as if confused at what Billy was doing. Billy wiggled he fingers at him.

"Bye bye."

Delbert resumed his charge, but he was too tall for the building, and he forgot to duck. His head slammed against a two-by-four rafter, which brought a squawk of pain and sent him tumbling back on his heels.

Billy didn't linger to listen to the string of cusses that Delbert was biting out. Slinging his bedroll across his back, he picked up his water and eggs and began to back slowly away as he listened to Delbert fighting to get the gate unlocked and open. Coming out of the gate, he looked wildly around, then spying Billy, he came barreling at him. Looking at the big man shuffle along, Billy, with a smile on his face, began to trot away.

The smile vanished; Delbert kicked his shoes off and came flying after Billy. With a yelp of fright, Billy stretched into full flight. The water jar in one hand and the bucket with the eggs in it, swinging in the other hand, put him at a great disadvantage; it slowed him down considerably. It was a good thing that Billy had had a decent head start, for he could hear the big man's footsteps gaining on him fast.

Up ahead, there was a ratty-looking mobile home with about a four-foot-high chain-link fence going all the way around it. Billy kept barreling toward the fence at full speed. Then like the maneuver he'd pulled on Mr. McPherson, the principal, in the last possible second, Billy, being small and quick, darted to his right. As he did, he felt a big hand brush his shirt collar, followed by a grunt, as Delbert plowed into the fence.

Billy took a quick look over his shoulder; the fence was close to being smashed flat, and Delbert was laying on it trying to untangle himself. Sprinting around the corner of the fence, he could hear the big guy already up and coming after him. Hanging on tight to his water and eggs, Billy climbed over the fence and went running across the yard. What frightened Billy most about the big man was that he never made a sound in his mad pursuit of him. Mr. McPherson had screamed, ranted, and cussed all the time he was chasing Billy.

Rolling his eyes toward heaven, Billy said, "You're supposed to be able to perform miracles. Why don't you perform one right now by throwing a hill up in front of me so I can outrun this madman?" Billy knew he didn't have time to wait for an answer, Delbert was over the fence and coming hard after him. Charging around the end of the single wide mobile home, he dashed for the back fence, hoping he could go over it and gain a few steps on the man chasing him. To his right he heard a gruff and low growl, and out of the corner of his eyes he saw a huge black dog coming out of a doghouse and joining in the chase for Billy. Billy thought to himself, *Everything in this part of the country seems to be big, and they all want a piece of me.*

Now for the first time, he heard Delbert make a sound. It was a startled yelp of surprise. Billy looked backward.

The big man had run right up on top of the big dog.

The dog and the man had forgotten all about Billy. Delbert was the one being pursued, as he fled in panic with the dog nipping at his heels. Billy had to stop and watch.

Delbert could have put some of those high-hurdle jumpers to shame the way he cleared that fence, and the dog cleared it just as easy.

There was the sound of a door opening in front of the house and a man yelling, "Rambo, get back here."

Boy, Billy thought, that must be one mean dog to be named Rambo. Delbert was still running, the black dog was still nipping at his heels, and the man was still yelling "Rambo!" as Billy went over the back fence and headed for safety.

"I suppose you're going to claim that that big dog was the hill you put up for me? Well, if you want to take credit for it, go ahead, but I'm not real sure myself."

Now he had to find a safe place so he could build a fire and cook his eggs; he was one hungry boy. He could see a row of tall trees a half mile or so in the distance; that would be an ideal place for him to stop and do his cooking.

Billy was having a few misgivings about dumping the manure in Martha's house. He felt that she had done him wrong for making him work to pay for spending a night on her cold old ground. But for some reason, he had kinda developed a liking for the big smiling woman. He was entering the trees now, so he put misgivings out of his mind.

He found a surprise in just a short distance. He came out of the trees, and he was standing on the bank of a wide, flowing river.

His hopes and spirits jumped; he had recalled driving alongside a river with Mr. and Mrs. Adams. As he recalled, it was a narrow, fast-moving stream, but he felt this had to be the same river. He knew that when a river changed its course, it also changed its nature. There was only one problem; he had to get on the other side, for that was the side they had been driving on.

But first, the eggs. He quickly gathered up some small twigs and branches and got a fire going. After the flame was well established, he placed some larger branches on it. Going to the river, he filled the bucket with the eggs in it half full of water. Setting it in the fire, he sat back and waited, enjoying the sound of the fire and the sound and view of the smooth flowing river. After what seemed forever, the water began to simmer then to boil. He sat patiently waiting; he knew it took a while to cook hard-boiled eggs.

As he was scanning the river, one small boat went down it; other than that, he saw no activity on the riverbanks or water. Finally he reached the point where he could no longer wait. He was starved. Sticking a small tree branch through the bail of the bucket so as to not to burn himself, he dumped the hot water out. Then carrying the bucket to the edge of the river, he dipped it full of cold water to cool the eggs off. They were cooked to perfection. He could have polished all six of them off, but he stopped at two. He was positive in his mind that he would be spending tomorrow night in the boys' home. But just to stay on the safe side, he would ration the eggs out two at a time. Now he had to figure out a way to cross that river. Picking up his belongings, he moved upriver. Hopefully he would find a bridge

BILLY YOU, NO MORE HILLS

to cross over on. After he walked for an hour, the river had stayed the same, and the sun was starting to dip to the west. He was determined to spend the night on the other side of the river.

Working his way through some trees that had grown right down to the water's edge, he came out into a clearing with a rundown old shack sitting in it. Billy hesitated, but he could see that it had been a long time since anyone had lived here.

Still, to be on the safe side, he cautiously approached the shack. Whoever had lived here or someone had junked out some old cars; pieces and parts were scattered all around the place.

From this location, he could see a long stretch of the river up ahead; it was still wide and smooth and with nobody in site.

He had to get across this river—how deep could it be? It was so wide and spread out. It was probably shallow all the way across. Heck, there was only one way to find out.

It was a warm and sunny day, and the water didn't appear to be cold. Without removing his clothes, he would just walk right out there a ways and see for himself just how deep the river was.

So thinking, he set his belongings on a tree stump close by and stepped out in the water. It went over his shoes. The water was cool, but it wasn't cold, so he moved farther out, one careful step at a time. Now the water was up to his knees, but it wasn't getting any deeper, as he moved farther and farther out. He looked back. He had traveled some distance out into the stream, with the water staying shallow. And up ahead as far as he could see, it didn't appear to be getting any deeper. Crossing this river was going to be easy. What if it did get up to his waist or even his armpits? That wouldn't be any problem for him. Going back to the shore, he gathered up his stuff. The first thing he did was form a pocket with one corner of his blanket. Placing the four remaining hard-boiled eggs in the pocket, he picked up a piece of wire from a pile of trash and tightly twisted it around the pocket holding the eggs. These eggs were all the food he was going to have before he reached the boys' home. And he wanted to take every precaution not to lose them.

Instead of slinging his bedroll across his back the way he had been carrying it, he draped it around his neck so it would ride higher.

He didn't mind getting wet, but he wanted to keep his bedding dry. Now he was ready. Stepping out into the river, he began his journey across.

He would be on the other side in plenty of time to dry out before the sun went down. The going was easy, and Billy was feeling good about himself. He had run into a lot of problems in his quest to get to the Mayhill Boys' Home. But he had conquered every one of them, and this river was going to be the easiest one of all.

Occasionally he would glance back over his shoulder. The shore behind was falling farther and farther behind, but the shoreline in front of him didn't seem to be getting closer. The next step Billy took, the water went up to his hips, causing him to hesitate for a fraction, then he moved on. He could handle this new depth and then some.

Yes, sirree, he would be stretched out in that warm sun shortly, drying out. Then he would eat two more of these good eggs. Then after a good night's sleep, he would polish off the two remaining eggs and go strolling down the road and through the gate. He couldn't wait to see the expressions on all their faces when he came strutting in.

Boy, was he going to have some tales to tell. At the exact moment, he looked back to see how far he had come. The bottom went out from underneath him.

Billy came up spitting out water and gasping for air. In a panic, he tried to turn back and find footing, but not only had he stepped off into deep water, he had also stepped into a swift current, which was pulling him downstream and away from the shallow water that he had been walking in. Billy could swim, but just enough to stay afloat.

The small town of Mayhill had a large indoor swimming pool, and one day out of each month, the orphans from the boys' home had the use of the pool, and that's where Billy learned to paddle and tread water. What he was in now was not a calm indoor swimming pool. It was a deep fast-moving river that was not only pulling him downstream, it was also trying to suck him under.

Trying to get his panic under control, Billy eased back on kicking and splashing. The river was much stronger than he was.

BILLY YOU, NO MORE HILLS

The only thing for him to do was ride the current whichever way it was going to take him and hope it was into the shallow water.

Billy's main concern were his clothes and bedroll. Their weight kept pulling him down, and he was fast becoming exhausted.

It would be easy enough for him to shed his bedroll, and with a little effort, he could shuck his clothes, but what a mess that would leave him in after he reached shore. It had yet to enter Billy's mind that he wouldn't make it. That he wouldn't escape from this river, and now to compound his woes, the chill from the water was beginning to seep into his body. Desperately he looked up. "Sir, I need help."

At times like this, he felt it paid to be polite. "Please, sir, I need another hill."

His struggles were getting weaker; his head was underwater more than it was above. It entered his head that he wasn't going to make it. He was going to drown in this cold relentless river, and nobody would ever know what had happened to him. And for some reason he didn't much understand, a picture of Redheaded Mary entered his mind. He would never get to see her again, and now, he wished he had told her that he might be in love with her.

He wouldn't lie to her by saying he was 100 percent sure he was in love with her because he still didn't know exactly how love was supposed to feel. The thought of the redheaded girl didn't stay with him long.

His strength was fast fading, and it took all his effort to keep his head above water. He felt that he had swallowed more water than was left in the river.

Then when he had about given up all hope, up ahead he could see something sticking up out of the water. Renewed hope seemed to give him a boost of power to reach whatever it was he could see. Now he could make it out; it was a dead tree protruding up out of the water.

The river seemed to be working in his favor at this moment, as it was pulling him in a straight course to intercept the large dead tree.

He was going to make it; he was going to escape from this river that had become a death trap.

The tree was coming up fast. Billy put all his effort into kicking his way to where he would bang into the dead tree and hang on for dear life. He didn't quite make it, but he was close enough to reach out with one hand and hang on.

He heaved a huge sigh of relief. He had escaped the river's death grip; he was safe. His sigh of relief was replaced with a moan of despair. The piece of bark his fingers had hooked into had come loose from the tree, and he was floating away once more in the river's death grip.

Billy gave up; there was no more fight left in him.

He could feel his bedroll being pulled from around his neck. Why try to save it? He wouldn't need it where he was going. Then he realized that the drag of the bedroll was slowing him down.

As the tail end of his blanket peeled off his shoulder, he made a desperate grab for it. His fingers hooked in the rope, and his downstream progress was stopped. He hung on for long moments, letting the water flow past him. The blanket was stretched taut from where it had snagged on the tree, and his weight was pulling against it.

The flow from the river had swung him around in front of the tree so the pressure was not nearly as strong as it had been. Letting the water run past him, Billy hung on to his bedroll, gathering his strength before making an effort to work his way up the snagged blanket to the safety of the tree.

He couldn't wait long; the cold water was sending a chill deeper and deeper into his body. He had to make his move now.

Slowly, hand over hand, he worked his way up the bedroll that he now thought of as his life line, all the while praying, *Please don't come loose, please don't come loose.* After what seemed like an eternity, moving his hands an inch at a time, his fumbling fingers found what the blanket had latched on to. It was a stub sticking out where a limb had broken off the tree.

With a tight grip on this, he eased himself around to the upstream side of the tree to where the river was pressing him tight against the tree. It was a big trunk, so he couldn't get his arms all the way around it, but he wrapped them as far around as he could.

BILLY YOU, NO MORE HILLS

After catching his breath for a while, he looked up. "I asked for a hill, and you sent me a big, mean dog. I asked for another hill, and you gave me a dead old tree. Well, you cut it pretty darn close both times. The next time I ask you for a hill, I wish you would speed it up somewhat."

And knowing you, you are probably going to claim that windmill was another hill you gave me. "Well, let me tell you, that was nip and tuck. Also, those dogs just about had me for their evening meal. So what I'm trying to tell you, when you see me in big trouble—which has been happening every darn day lately—don't just sit up there enjoying the show. Jump in and give me a hand. OK?"

Billy thought that maybe he had better shut up before the old boy up there got upset with him and held the hill back even longer next time.

After resting there for a while, with the water gently bumping him back and forth against the tree. Billy planned his next move. He had to get up in this tree so that he would be dried out before the sun went down.

Directly above his head was a sturdy-looking tree limb. It was low enough for him to reach. Grabbing hold of it with his both hands, he fumbled around with his foot until he found the stub that his bedroll had latched on to. Making sure he was secure, he released his grip from the tree limb with his left hand, and cautiously bending down, he took hold of his bedroll and unhooked it from where it had latched on to the tree. Pulling it up, he draped the soggy mess over the limb he was hanging on to.

This tree that had come to his rescue was big, and overhead within an easy climb; there were two very large limbs growing out from the trunk. A good secure, safe place for Billy to wedge himself into.

Trailing the dripping blanket behind him, he worked his way up and, heaving a sigh, eased himself back against the trunk.

The last few nights had been spent in some weird places, and this night he would be perched in a tree like some big bird.

He spread his blanket out over some branches so it would dry out before nightfall.

Leaning back against the tree trunk with the warm sun beating down on him, Billy dozed off.

Once more, he dreamed that he was back in the home, asleep on his cot in his own private hallway. And in his dream there was a motor running, making a loud noise, and there were people shouting and laughing and making all kinds of racket, and he couldn't understand why Mrs. Jamison was letting all this commotion go on. She had always run a tight ship. After lights out, no sounds of any kind was allowed.

How in the world did she expect a fellow to sleep with all this going on? The motor sound and the laughing and shouting was still going on.

Billy woke with a start. The sun was dropping below the horizon in a beautiful red sunset. The motor sound and the laughing and shouting was still going on.

A motorboat was a short way from where Billy was perched in his tree. It was slowly putting its way down the river, and the half dozen or so people on board were having a merry old time.

Billy began moving his arms and shouting at the top of his lungs. His voice was drowned out by the merrymakers on the boat, and his frantic, waving arms went unnoticed. Dejectedly he sat back down. If he hadn't fallen asleep, he would have seen the boat in time to attract their attention.

Hunger pains made him think of the four remaining eggs. He doubted very much if they had survived the ordeal he had just went through. Pulling the blanket, which was completely dry, from the branch where it had been hanging, his fumbling hands found the pocket he had made for the eggs. To his surprise they had fared well in the wild ride down the river. Three of the eggs had cracked shells but not overly cracked; the fourth had come through fully intact. And surprisingly, the salt in his shaker came out in good shape.

He ate the two eggs that had received the most damage. It took a lot of willpower to keep from eating the other two. But common sense prevailed. He did not know how long he would be stuck in this tree before someone came to his rescue.

BILLY YOU, NO MORE HILLS

The sun was down, and darkness was fast coming on. Even though Billy had had a nap, he was still tired from his ordeal.

To be on the safe side, Billy removed the rope from his bedroll and wrapped it around the tree trunk and himself. He then tied a secure knot. He didn't want to wake up in the grip of that cold river again.

It was very uncomfortable to sleep in the position that he was in.

Chapter 9

All through the long night, Billy kept waking up with starts, each time trying to wiggle his cramped body into a more comfortable position, but there was none. Once more, like on other mornings, the hot sun beating down on him woke Billy.

Trying to stretch out, he gave out a groan. He was sore from head to foot from the beating the river had given him.

Untying himself from the tree, he put his bedroll back together.

Standing up where he could really stretch out, Billy looked up the river, and there, right before his eyes, a big boat was bearing down on him.

He grabbed up his blanket and, wildly waving it back and forth, began to shout at the top of his lungs.

He was seen; there were two men standing on the front of the boat, and one of them was pointing at Billy.

Billy could hear the boat's engine slowing down, and the boat came drifting his way. He quickly rolled up his bedroll and slung it over his shoulder.

He was saved. But what plausible explanation could he give these people for being in this dead old tree out in the middle of a river?

The boat was swinging in close to the tree. A man in some kind of a sailor suit had a long rod with a point on the end in his hands, and as the boat eased up to the tree, he stuck the point of the rod into the tree to hold the boat back.

BILLY YOU, NO MORE HILLS

People were lined up along the boat rail, staring at him with their mouths open. Billy thought, *This is how monkeys must feel when people come to the zoo to stare at them in their cages.* Billy noticed that all of them were older folks. This must be a senior citizen tour. Now a big man in a captain's uniform, with his arms folded across his chest, shouted at Billy, "Boy, what the hell are you doing out here, and how in God's name did you get here?"

In one breath the man had cussed, and in the next breath, he had used God's name. He would like to see how Mrs. Jamison would handle this fellow.

He couldn't think what to tell them, so he blurted out, "Well, sir, I started across this river yesterday afternoon, and it got dark on me, so I stopped and spent the night here in this tree."

There was stunned silence from the boat. Billy chuckled to himself. That answer had sure set them back on their heels.

While Billy was chuckling to himself, someone on the boat started laughing. All the people that Billy could see besides the captain and some of his crew were old folks. But the laughter sounded like it was coming from a lady, a young lady.

He tried to pick her out of the crowd so he could give her a mean look. But he couldn't spot her. "Boy, are you going to jump on board here, or are you going to spend the rest of your life in that tree?"

Then Billy felt that he asked the stupidest question that he had ever asked in his life. "Which way are you going?"

There came that laughter again; this time he spotted her. She was one of the prettiest ladies that he had ever seen.

He gave her his meanest look. She put her hand to her mouth, but it didn't stop her from laughing.

The Captain bellowed, "Good Christ Almighty, boy, you can see what the hell direction we're going. I don't have all day, so get your butt on board, or I'll sure as hell go off and leave you."

Yep, this man would be blowing soap bubbles for a month.

Billy waited until the boat rocked his way. He jumped, his feet catching the edge of the deck, and his hands grabbed the top railing.

The captain, standing in front of Billy with his hands on his hips, spoke up. "Boy, I don't know who the hell you are, and I sure as hell don't know what you were doing in that tree. 'Now you go back there someplace and find a hole to sit in, and don't let me catch you pestering these folks who are trying to have a nice morning cruise."

Yeah, Billy thought, *as if I'm the one stopping them from having a pleasant cruise. It's probably the other way around. It's not every day you find a kid setting in a tree in the middle of a river. Heck, this will give the old people something to tell their friends and talk about for a whole month.*

Benches lined the rail around the boat, and these benches were occupied by these older men and women on their morning pleasure cruise, and each and every one of them was staring at him as if he had been plucked off Mars instead of out of a tree. Moving to the far side of the boat, he came face-to-face with the pretty young lady that had laughed at him.

She was sitting by herself, and there was an empty seat beside her. She patted it, meaning for him to sit beside her. She wasn't laughing, but there was a big smile on her face. Billy looked around, hoping to find someplace else to sit, but all the benches were occupied. He looked back at her. She patted the bench again and said, "Please." He reluctantly moved over and sat down beside her.

All was quiet for a while, then she asked him, "What's your name?"

"Billy"

"Billy what?"

"Just Billy, just plain old Billy."

He was through telling people his last name was You and being laughed at.

The lady went "Oh! You don't have a last name?"

"No, ma'am. I'm an orphan, and I don't have a first name either. Billy is a name someone threw at me so I would know when I was being talked to."

He put the part about Billy in so the pretty lady would feel ashamed of herself for laughing at a poor orphan boy. It seemed to work, for she said. "Billy, I'm sorry I laughed at you, but you stopped and spent the night in that tree, like you would a motel?" And darn if she didn't start laughing again.

Then the absurdity of it hit him, and he was laughing right along with her.

When they finished their laugher, she asked, "Why were you out there?"

"Aw, I was stupid. That darn river didn't look deep. I thought that I could wade right across it. Boy, was I wrong. I just about drowned my fool self."

He could see real concern in her eyes, and she patted him on the hand in sympathy.

"It must have been terrible for you, trapped out there all night by yourself."

Billy threw out his chest; for some reason he wanted to impress this lady. "No, ma'am, it wasn't so bad. I've been in worse places."

She smiled at his statement; it was such a nice smile that he didn't resent it.

"My name is Elly, Elly Morgan. I'm not old enough to be called *ma'am* yet." She stuck out her hand. "You call me Elly, and I'll call you Billy—is that a deal?"

He started to say "Yes, ma'am," which made them both laugh again.

He was really starting to like this lady named Elly. It brought Redheaded Mary to mind. He sure hoped he wasn't being untrue to the redheaded girl.

Elly was asking him another question. "You said you were an orphan, did you ever know your father and mother?"

He shook his head. "No."

"Did you ever think about trying to find them?"

Billy thought a moment. "Yes, when I was eight years old, I ran away from the home. I thought they were mistreating me. They weren't. The home is a nice place. I had been thinking about my mother a lot and wondering what she was like. So I ran away to find her." He laughed. "I didn't hardly get out the gate before they caught me. That's the last time I went looking for her."

"If you had found her, how would you have known it was her?"

"Well, I don't know, but I think she would have been about as pretty as you." Billy didn't know how in the world he had let that slip out. He was going to have to learn to get better control of his mouth.

Elly's arms went around him in a big hug. "Billy, that's sweet. That's the nicest compliment I've had in my whole life." Billy's eyes darted up and down the boat, hoping no one had seen what had went on. A boy his age was too old to be hugged by a woman.

Thank goodness none of the other passengers seemed to have noticed the hug. He didn't like to admit it, but the hug felt pretty darn nice. From day 1, when Billy had ran away from the school and the Adamses' home, he had been hungry. Being hungry had become part of his life. He had accepted that and didn't dwell on it too much.

As he was sitting there on this rocking boat next to this young woman that he was beginning to like very much, he thought of the two remaining eggs and realized how hungry he really was.

Undoing his bedroll, he fished out the eggs. Elly had been watching what he was doing. He showed her the eggs. "I haven't had breakfast yet. I guess I had better eat so I can keep up my strength." She was looking at him kind of funny, he thought, but she nodded her head.

As he began peeling the egg that was somewhat cracked up, he realized that he was being very selfish. "Here, I have two of them. I'll share one with you." He held out the uncracked egg to Elly.

"No, no, Billy, if you are going to keep that strength up, you need to eat both of them. Thank you, it was very nice of you to offer one to me."

Billy shook his head. "No, if one person has something and another person doesn't have something, then the person that has something should share it with the person who doesn't have anything."

To Billy, what he said didn't seem to make any sense. He hoped she understood what he meant. She must have; she took the egg he was offering her. Looking at him with a real serious look in her eyes, she brought the egg up and cracked it against her forehead, saying, "That's the way you crack a hard-boiled egg."

It startled Billy so bad he burst out laughing. They sat there like two fools laughing their heads off.

BILLY YOU, NO MORE HILLS

Billy couldn't believe a grown woman would crack an egg on her forehead. At the home, if you got caught cracking an egg that way, you would get banged on the forehead with a knife handle or a spoon.

Brushing off her hands, Elly said, "Billy, I do believe that is the best egg that I have ever eaten. Did you cook them yourself?"

"Yep, I sure did."

"Well, they were delicious. Where did you get them?"

"I worked for them."

He thought that he had better leave it at that. Besides, it wasn't really a lie. He had cleaned out the chicken pen—or most of it anyway. She stood up. "Come on, we're getting ready to dock."

He was disappointed. The boat was docking on the same side of the river that he had started his ill-fated trip from.

He wished the trip down the river had been a little longer; he would have liked to spend more time with Elly.

The boat came to a stop, bumping up against the dock.

There was a lot of scurrying around as the crew anchored the boat down and the passengers began disembarking.

Elly put her hand on his arm, holding him back. "Let's give these old folks time to get off first." With lots of shuffling along, holding on to the rails and each other, with Elly and Billy bringing up the rear.

Billy was at a loss. What should he do—go up the river to where he had been then keep hoping to find a bridge to cross? Or go downriver hoping to find a bridge? Going downriver he would be getting farther and farther away from the Mayhill Boys' Home. So upstream it would be.

As Billy stepped off the ramp onto the boat dock, the captain, with arms folded across his chest, was standing there waiting for him.

"Boy, I don't know where you belong, but it's not around here. So you just light a shuck on down the road."

Before Billy could move or speak, Elly was standing nose-to-nose with the boat captain.

"Captain Hoyle, you back off right now. Billy's with me."

"Miss Morgan, I can't allow it."

Billy couldn't believe what he saw—how a little woman could bully such a big man. Placing her hand on his chest, she pushed the Captain back a step.

"You can't allow? I'll tell you what you can allow. You can allow yourself to get back on your little boat and go putt-putting back up the river, or tomorrow there will be a new captain doing it for you."

"I'm sorry, Miss Morgan. I didn't mean to get out of line." As he was speaking, the captain hurriedly backed up the ramp.

Elly stood staring at him until he was out of sight. Billy didn't ever remember seeing such fire in a person's eyes.

Billy had been the champion of the smaller boys at the home. Now it looked like he had his own champion.

Elly was back to her old sweet self. Looking at him with a smile on her face, she said, "I guess I told him how the cow ate the cabbage, didn't I?"

Billy didn't know what she meant by that remark, but he agreed. "You sure did."

She took him by the hand and said, "Come on, let's go get you settled in." Billy looked to see where she was leading him; he couldn't believe the place. It was a huge building, three stories high, with row up on row of windows. There was a big parking lot full of fancy cars, and past that a tennis court, four deep and people playing tennis in each court.

On three sides of the big complex, there were golf courses with men and women on it swinging golf clubs. Billy held back.

"What's wrong, Billy?"

"What kind of a place is this?"

She smiled at the question. "It's a country club, Rock Creek Country Club."

"What do people do here?"

"Well, they live here, they play here, they enjoy life here. It's a private club, you have to be a member to come here."

"Well, I kinda don't think I belong here, not being a member and all, so I had better do what the Captain said, get on out of here before I get in trouble."

Elly was shaking her head. "You will do no such thing. I'm a paid-up member, and you're with me, and that's that." Sure sounded final to Billy. He reluctantly let her lead him up some wide steps and through some equally wide doors into a huge room. Everything about this place was mammoth. The room was filled with comfortable chairs and couches with men and women sitting in them, reading newspapers or magazines.

They all stopped reading or whatever they were doing and watched Elly leading this boy across the floor, a boy with faded and worn clothes and a bedroll slung across his back. They had to be thinking Huck Finn had come back to life, and this Huck Finn boy was wishing a hole would open up and swallow him. It didn't happen.

Elly with Billy in tow, marched up to a long counter with a young man behind it. Giving the counter a loud slap, Elly said, "Good morning, Arthur!"

"Good morning, Miss Morgan. Can I help you?"

About that time, his eyes came to rest on Billy, and he got a startled look on his face. Pointing his finger at Billy, he asked, "Miss Morgan, what is this?"

Elly looked around at Billy and acted surprised that he was there. "Well, I believe it's a boy." She winked at Billy. "Are you a boy?" Billy knew that she was making fun of the clerk for asking a silly question.

"Yes, ma'am, I'm a boy."

Elly laughed, then she got serious. "Arthur, this is my little brother, Billy. He's going to be staying with me for a while. So I'll be moving out of my room into the executive suite." Billy couldn't believe that Elly had told this guy that he, Billy, was her brother.

Arthur was stammering, "Miss…Miss Morgan, the executive suite is reserved."

"Well, you can unreserve it. Billy and I are moving in."

"Miss Morgan." Arthur was pleading now. "I'll lose my job."

"OK, OK. Arthur, get your so-called manager out here."

With a big sigh of relief, Arthur said, "Yes, ma'am" and punched some numbers on a phone. There was a short delay, then Arthur spoke into the phone.

"Mr. Hoyle, sir, I think you should come out here."

Hanging up the phone, he looked at Elly. "He will be right out, Miss Morgan."

Elly leaned on the counter. "Right out had better mean a few minutes. I don't have all day." Elly gave Billy another wink; she seemed to be enjoying herself. He wished she would back off and go a little easy on these people before she got them both kicked out.

A big man with a head full of gray hair in a business suit and tie and a very stern look on his face came out of a door that said Business Manager on it.

The stern look vanished, and he stopped in midstride and glanced back over his shoulder as if looking for an escape route when he saw who was there waiting for him.

With a forced smile on his face and rubbing his hands together, he asked, "Miss Morgan, how can I help you?" Then his eyes fell on Billy. "What have we here?"

Once more, Elly looked down at Billy. He could see laughter in her eyes, but she asked him very seriously, "What did you say you were?"

Billy didn't know what else to do but go along with her. "A boy."

"Elmer, this is my little brother, Billy. Billy and I will be moving into the executive suite."

Elmer wrung his hands some more. "Miss Morgan, the executive suite is reserved. I can't let you have it."

This time Elly didn't use the man's first name, and her voice was no longer friendly. "Mr. Hoyle, who reserved it?"

"Mr. Harry Potts."

"Harry Potts, why that pompous ass. He doesn't need two rooms. Billy and I do. When old Harry gets here, send him to me if he gives you any trouble."

Elly looked around. "Where's the bellboy?" She spied one. "Jimmy, get your butt over here."

A tall, gangly teenage boy came running over. "Yes, Miss Morgan?"

"Jimmy, how many times have I told you that I'm not old enough for you to call me ma'am or Miss Morgan?" Jimmy looked

BILLY YOU, NO MORE HILLS

over at the two men behind the counter, and there was a smirk on his face as if to say "You two have to call her Miss Morgan, I don't."

"Sorry, Elly, what can I do for you?"

"Jimmy, I would like for you to meet my brother, Billy."

Jimmy stuck out his hand. "Hi, Billy." Billy shook the offered hand.

Elly headed for a bank of doors that said Elevator above them. "Come on, you two, we've got some moving to do."

She pushed a button, and some doors slid open. Billy followed the other two in. He had never been on an elevator before, so he was a little apprehensive, but his fears were unfounded. The ride was very smooth; he enjoyed it.

The elevator stopped at the third floor; the doors slid open. Billy followed Elly and Jimmy down a hall to the first door on the right. Elly inserted a card in a slot, and Billy heard the door locks open. He shook his head. At the home there had been very few locked doors, and the ones that were used the old-fashioned keys to open them.

Elly put the two boys to work. In a short time, they had moved her from her present room to one across the hall, which turned out to be two rooms. Elly stored her belongings in the front room, then led him into the second room. "This is your room. What do you think?"

As he walked around the room, he didn't know what to think. The far wall was all windows looking out over the golf course. There was a huge bathroom with a separate tub and shower and double sinks. The bed Billy felt was big enough to get lost in. And there was enough closet space to hang up all the clothes the boys at the home owned.

He sank into a big, comfortable chair. Elly moved over and placed her hand on Billy's shoulder. "Billy, what is wrong?"

Billy looked up at her. "A few nights ago, I slept in an old rusty truck. The next night, I slept on top of a windmill in a real bad storm, with a pack of wild dogs down on the ground, wanting to eat me. The third night, I slept in some bushes, hiding from two hobos who were wanting a piece of my hide. The fourth night, I slept alongside a wooden fence trying to stay warm and was woken up by a giant kicking me in the side. And you know where I slept last night?

In an old dead tree in the middle of a river that tried to drown me." He pointed to the bed. "Now look where I'm going to sleep tonight." Billy looked up and spoke out loud. "Mister, I think you're playing games with me."

Jimmy was standing there with his mouth open, not knowing whether to believe Billy's wild tale or not. He could tell by Elly's expression that she did.

Elly took hold of Billy's hand and pulled him out of the chair. "Come on, let's go downtown and get something to eat. That hard-boiled egg you gave me this morning is long gone, and when we get back, you and I are going to sit down, and you are going to tell me about your adventures."

Elly took hold of Jimmy's hand and slapped a folded-up bill in it.

"Thank you for your help, Jimmy." Jimmy went out the door with a big smile on his face. "You're welcome, Elly."

Elly turned to Billy. "I'm going to take a quick shower and change my clothes, then you and I are going to get something to eat and go shopping for you some new clothes."

Billy tugged at his pants and shirt. "We don't have to do that. These are still pretty good, this is my best pair." Then he realized and had to laugh. "Heck, this is my only pair."

Darned if she didn't put her arms around him and give him another hug. "Billy, those clothes are a disgrace. We're going shopping and get you all spiffed up real fancy. I'll be ready in a flash."

Dropping back down in the chair, Billy closed his eyes. The next thing he knew, Elly was shaking him. "Wake up, Billy, we've got things to do." Billy struggled out of his sleep. He hadn't had a good night's sleep since he had run away, and it had finally caught up with him.

Elly had changed her clothes and fixed her hair differently. There was no doubt in Billy's mind that Elly was the prettiest lady he had ever seen. A twang of guilt shot through him as he thought of Redheaded Mary. The redheaded girl could stand shoulder to shoulder with Elly as far as looks were concerned.

"Come on, Billy, get a hussle on, let's go." As Elly was walking away from him toward the door, he noticed the blue jeans she had on. They fit her so tight he wondered how in the world she had gotten them on.

When they got back, he might just have to sit her down and have a talk with her that there was no excuse for a lady to wear clothes that tight.

Down in the lobby, Elly looked around, not seeing what she wanted. She went over and hopped up on the clerk's receiving counter. Reaching down behind the counter, she picked up a mike. Speaking into it, she said. "Jimmy, Jimmy, come out wherever you are. Get your skinny butt in here. I need you."

Billy looked around, shocked at the way Elly did things and the words she used. The other people in the lobby seemed to think the same way as Billy. They had all stopped what they were doing and were staring at Elly where she sat on the counter. Arthur, the clerk, had moved back away from Elly as far as he could, and if she had shouted "Boo" at him, he probably would have vaulted from the room.

From a hallway, Jimmy came running into the room.

Elly hopped off the counter and flipped him some keys. "Boy! Fetch my car."

With a big smile on his face, Jimmy made a wide, sweeping bow. "Yes, Your Highness, right away."

This brought laughter from Elly. But no one else in the room seemed amused.

Billy followed Elly out the door. As they reached the bottom of the steps, a small red convertible sports car came flying around the corner of the building. It came to a screeching stop. Jimmy jumped out and, while holding the door open, made another sweeping bow. "Your vehicle, madam!"

As Elly got in the driver's side, she handed Jimmy another folded-up bill.

Billy thought to himself, *Boy, she sure is free with her money.*

Billy settled into the passenger side of the car, and Jimmy patted him on the shoulder. "Buckle up, Billy, you're going to need it."

Billy found out in a hurry what Jimmy meant. Elly popped the clutch, and the little car shot forward, snapping Billy's head back against the seat.

They went flying out of the driveway and onto the road.

In a short distance, they came to a dam across the river.

Now Billy knew why the river had been so wide where he had tried to cross. People were out on the dam. Some were strolling along; others were leaning on the protective railing looking over the side at the river far below.

The road was going down, becoming steeper and steeper with one curve right after another. There were huge round boulders on both sides of the road, and once in a while, you could catch a view of the river far below. Instead of slowing up when they came into the curves, Elly increased the speed of the little red car.

Each bend in the road they went around, Billy could hear the tires screeching on the pavement. Elly had both hands on the steering wheel; her hair was blowing straight back, and she had a smile on her face. Billy could tell she was enjoying this very much. For him, he felt that he would be safer back in the river.

Thank goodness it wasn't a long drive. They came whipping around a final curve, and there was a small town sitting before them with a sign that said Rock Creek.

The first cross street they came to, Elly made a screeching left-hand turn. The next street they came to, she did the same thing, making another screeching left turn. They came to a braking stop in front of a building that said Rock Creek Cafe.

After getting out of the car, Billy looked around. Across the street from the café was the police station.

That made him nervous, and across the street from the police station and caddy corner from the café was Rock Creek Hospital.

Before Billy could do any further looking, Elly said, "Come on, let's grab a bite to eat, then we've got some shopping to do."

She went charging through the swinging front door, with Billy right behind her. Everything this woman did, she seemed to do in a hurry. It was a small café on the inside with tables scattered about, with about half of them occupied. Across the room was a counter with one man sitting at the far end. There were eight stools all told, along the counter. Elly, without slowing her pace, went across the room and plopped down on the nearest end stool.

BILLY YOU, NO MORE HILLS

Billy sat on the one next to her. She had no more than sat down when she gave the countertop three or four ringing slaps and shouted, "All right, let's have some service down this way. We don't have all day."

Billy flinched at this going on. Elly was the most demanding person he had ever met. About this time, Billy took a quick look over his shoulder to make sure an escape route was open. Because by the time Elly had finished her shouting and pounding on the counter, a huge round man came striding out of a door, back of the counter. His huge head was smoothly bald; he had thick black bushy eyebrows and a full curly black beard. He was drying his hands on a dirty-looking apron that Billy thought must have been made from a bedsheet; the man's belly was so big around. The big fellow headed straight to where Billy and Elly were sitting, and he had a mean, mad look on his face.

Billy eased himself to the edge of the stool, ready to bolt. Elly had brought this down on them; she would have to fend for herself.

The big man stopped when his round belly hit the counter. Placing his hands on his hips, he glared at Elly.

Billy was still ready to run, but he felt a little pride being here with Elly. For she didn't flinch or move back an inch. She just sat there, glaring right back at the big man. Then to Billy's horror, she raised up off her stool and, bending over the counter, using her finger, she poked the big man in his big round belly and said, "Fred, you've been eating out. You didn't get a gut like that eating the slop you serve here."

The big man's arms came over the counter and went around Elly. Billy didn't know if he should try and save her or run for the door and save himself.

Then to Billy's surprise, Elly's arms went around the big guy's neck, and she was hugging him right back. They were both laughing, and the big man spoke.

"Elly, I'm sure glad to see you back. This is a dull place when you're not around."

Then all the other customers in the room had joined in the laugher, and they were all shouting greetings at her. Like "Welcome back Elly!",

"Glad you're back, Elly!",

"It's about time you came home, Elly!" and other remarks like that.

Elly swiveled around on her stool and was waving and throwing kisses at her audience. Swiveling back around, she slapped the counter again and shouted down to the waitress at the far end, talking to the customers sitting there.

"Mary, quit flirting with Josh there. He's old enough to be your father. Besides that, he's married and has four kids at home. Now come on down here and give us some service. Billy looked at the lady Elly had called Mary. She was pretty but nowhere near as pretty as his Redheaded Mary. This made Billy blush, thinking of Redheaded Mary as his.

The waitress Mary talked with Josh a while longer then slowly moved down the counter and stopped in front of Billy.

"Can I help you, sir?"

Elly spoke up. "We'll both have the deluxe hamburger, a large fry, and a large chocolate shake.

"Miss, I'll get to you in a moment, this young gentleman comes first."

Billy's eyes got big as he waited for Elly to explode. Instead, to his surprise, she demurely folded her hands on the counter and, in a small voice, like she had been put down, said, "Sorry, ma'am."

Then once more to Billy's surprise, both women burst out laughing and hugging each other over the counter like they were long-lost sisters.

After the laughing and hugging was over, Mary stepped back and, with hands on hips and a stern look on her face, said to Elly, "I knew you were back long before you got here. I heard you pull out of the driveway at the Club, and I could hear your tires screeching in protest all the way down the hill. You had better learn to slow that toy that you call a car down before you kill yourself."

BILLY YOU, NO MORE HILLS

Elly laughed, waving her hand as if brushing the accusation aside.

Billy didn't laugh. "You sure do, you even drive faster than that. I might have to just walk back up the hill." That brought laughter from everyone in the room, which embarrassed Billy, then embarrassing him even more, Elly reached over and hugged him, saying, "Mary, I would like you to meet my brother, Billy."

Being introduced as her brother, Billy liked that. He just didn't think it was proper for a twelve-year-old boy to be hugged by a woman.

The food came, and Billy could not remember eating a meal that was so delicious. Of course, maybe the reason the food tasted so good was because his meals lately had been few and far between.

Elly patted his shoulder. "If you're still hungry, we'll get you another order?"

Billy rubbed his stomach. "Nope, that will hold me for a while."

"Good, let's get out of here and go buy you some new duds."

Over at the cash register, Billy got embarrassed for Elly. She seemed to be making a spectacle of herself. She was twisting around and jumping up and down, all the while trying to get a hand in a pocket of her tight-fitting jeans. Two older men in a booth close by started teasing her and making fun of her.

"Elly," one of them said, "you're going to have to go on a diet and lose some weight so you want have so much trouble getting your money out of your pocket."

The other man piped up, "Heck, she doesn't have to lose weight. All she has to do is buy a pair of pants about four sizes bigger."

This exchange brought another round of laughter from the customers in the room.

Billy could not believe Elly's responses. She didn't seem to have any shame. She bent over and stuck her rear end out at the two men and wiggled it back and forth.

"You two are just jealous that you don't look as good in your clothes as I do in mine."

This brought some hand claps, and one of the old men answered, "That's a fact, Elly, that's a fact."

Yep, Billy thought. When the right opportunity came up, he was going to sit her down and have a long talk with her. Explain to her in a nice way that wearing her clothes skintight just didn't look proper. And as for wiggling her rear end at men, that was unladylike.

Everyone in the café shouted, "Good-bye, Elly!" as Billy and Elly went out the door.

Billy followed Elly up the street a ways and into a door on a building. Its sign over the door said Rock Creek Clothing.

Inside, an older lady came to meet them, and she and Elly went into a hugging match. If Mrs. Jamison had these people in the home for a little while, she would put a stop to this hugging nonsense.

Elly told the lady what they wanted and helped Billy pick out some new clothes. Going into a dressing room, he changed into a pair of dark-blue pants and a white shirt. Coming out of the dressing room, he was led over to the shoe department and fitted with new socks and a fancy pair of dress shoes.

Next, Elly held some ties against his shirt, and she and the store lady decided which one would look best on him. Elly put the tie on for him, then after adjusting his collar and smoothing and patting his shirt down, she stepped back and, putting her hands together, said, "Billy, you are one handsome young man." She pointed. "Take a look for yourself."

There was a full-length mirror; Billy had never seen himself in one before. All the mirrors at the home were small and faded and most of them cracked. About all they were good for was to look into and comb your hair.

Self-consciously, Billy stood in front of the mirror and viewed himself. Elly was right; he was indeed a fine-looking boy. Now he could understand why Redheaded Mary liked him, why she was always winking at him, and why she had kissed him. Yep, he was one fine-looking kid. He sure hoped that he hadn't broken the redheaded girl's heart by running away like he had. Elly bought him two complete sets of clothes, right down to socks and shoes.

Billy could just see himself, walking into the Mayhill Boys' Home with these fancy duds on, tie and all, and carrying another complete set of new clothes with him. It would knock their eyes out

BILLY YOU, NO MORE HILLS

and set them back on their heels, seeing what a success he had made of himself.

Then he would get all of them into the mess hall and sit them down and tell them about his adventures and troubles and dangers trying to get back to the home. Of course he would be modest and humble in the telling, like it was an everyday thing with him—handling those dangerous and trying situations that he had been through and handling them with ease and bravery.

Elly slowed her driving down somewhat on the way back to the country club. Parking in front of the building, she turned to Billy.

"What kind of a grade are you going to give me on my drive back?"

He sat there like he was giving it some deep thought then told her, "I'll give you a B or maybe a B-."

Elly jumped out of the car. "Good, I'll settle for that."

Inside, Elly let out a yell, "Jimmy, where are you?"

From across the room, he yelled back, "Over here."

With her car keys in her hand, Elly went into a baseball pitcher's elaborate windup with a big high kick and let the keys fly. Jimmy snagged them out of the air, and Elly told him, "Park my car, boy."

Jimmy gave another sweeping bow—"Yes, ma'am"—and went lopping out the door.

Billy glanced around. There was a few people in the lobby and Arthur, the clerk, behind the desk. And Billy could tell by the expressions on their faces that they were not amused by Elly and Jimmy's antics.

He was ready to go up to their room, but she stood there with her arms crossed, tapping her foot and staring at a clock hanging on the far wall. Inside of two, maybe three, minutes, Jimmy came charging back into the building and to a stop in front of Elly. She pointed to the clock that she had been staring at. "What took you so long, boy?"

Jimmy bowed his head. "I'm not as young as I used to be, ma'am."

"That's no excuse, I'll overlook it this time." Once more, she stuck her hand in a pocket of her tight-fitting pants and went into

CLARENCE W. LESLIE

her wiggling, squirming, and jumping-up-and-down routine. Billy looked around and felt embarrassment for Elly. The rest of the people in the room were staring at her as she went through her multiple gyrations. Finally, in triumph, she pulled out a ten-dollar bill, and to Billy's big-eyed surprise, she handed it to laughing Jimmy. Billy had never owned ten dollars in his entire life, and here Jimmy had earned ten dollars for about three minutes' work.

Right then, Billy decided that as soon as he was old enough, this was the place he would go to work at. Heck, in no time he would be rich.

Elly was talking. "Jimmy, what are you laughing at."

Still laughing, Jimmy pointed at her. "You."

Elly spread out her hands. "Is it my fault that they make pockets so small anymore?"

"No, but I'm sure glad."

Elly slapped him on the shoulder. "You've got a nasty mind, get out of here. Come on, Billy, lets go to our room."

On the elevator Billy was quiet, thinking about what he was going to say to her concerning the type of clothes she wore and the way she and Jimmy made fools of themselves in the lobby.

Once inside their rooms, Elly gave him his opening. "Billy, is something wrong? You're awful quiet."

He threw back his shoulders. "Yes, Elly, there is—we need to talk."

Elly walked over and sat down on the edge of her bed and patted a spot beside her. "Come over here and sit beside me, and we will talk about it."

Billy hesitated. He didn't think that it was proper to sit on the same bed that there was a lady sitting on. Why, if that was Redheaded Mary sitting there on the bed, he would just have to get up and leave the room. Nope, it just wasn't proper for a boy to be in the same bedroom where a girl was at.

Elly patted the bed again. "Billy!" There was a stern sound to her voice, telling that he had better sit down. Sliding to the end of the bed, he sat down as far away from her as he could get.

105

BILLY YOU, NO MORE HILLS

Elly slapped the spot beside her, and this time, there was a command in her voice. "Here beside me, Billy—now!" He moved over next to her, and to his chagrin, she took hold of his hand and squeezed it. Now he was not only sitting on a bed with a woman, he was also holding hands with her. There was probably a law or a rule some place that said you weren't supposed to do things like this. Thank goodness they were behind closed doors, where no one could see what was going on.

In a soft voice, Elly asked, "Tell me what's bothering you, Billy."

He hesitated, not really knowing how to put his feelings into words.

"Come on," she prodded him. "If you don't tell me what's wrong, we will never get it straightened out."

He took a dry breath. "All right, I'll tell you. We go to Rock Creek and everyone seems to love you. They hug you and kid with you and cut up with you and all that kind of stuff." He looked at her. "Then we come back here, and none of these folks seem to like you." She looked at him with big solemn eyes and nodded for him to go on.

"Well, maybe it's because you give these people here such a rough time. And then there's the way you and Jimmy carry on." Then in a stern voice of his own, he said, "I think it would be better if you didn't do that anymore."

He held his breath waiting for her reaction. Elly sat there nodding her head back and forth, as if in deep thought, pondering the things he had told her. She heaved a big sigh. "Is there anything else?"

He heaved a big sigh in return. "Yes." He had to let her know, so he blurted it out. "Maybe you shouldn't wear such tight-fitting clothes."

Elly looked at him with a startled look on her face. Then she let out a squeal of her girlish laugher. Flopping back on the bed, she began kicking her legs up and down, all the while laughing her fool head off. Or so Billy thought; as quickly as she had flopped down, Elly sat up, and to Billy's surprise and shock, she put her arms around him and gave him a big hug.

If word of him sitting on a bed with a woman with her hugging him ever got out, his reputation would be ruined forever. He wished he had never tried talking to her. She removed her arms from around him and asked, "Is that all that bothering you, or is there more?"

He shook his head. "No, that's all." She heard a big sigh.

"All right, I'll answer the best I can. First off, the clothes I wear when I'm with you won't be those skintight pants we well-built shapely women like to show off in."

This statement jolted Billy straight and jerked his eyes and mouth wide open. He must have looked like a fool sitting there and staring at her like that.

Apparently he did. Elly flopped back on the bed and let out another one of her wild girlish squeals of laughter. Sitting back up, she patted him on the knee. "I'm sorry, Billy, I was teasing you. I always tease the ones I love." Christ, here he was, just a twelve-year-old boy, and he already had a girl his age and a grown woman in love with him. He guessed that was the penalty you had to pay for being the good-looking boy that he was.

She was talking again. "Now about this second problem concerning the folks that like or dislike me. First, the people in Rock Creek. I went to school there. I've known most of them all my life. They are all my dear friends, and I love them dearly."

Christ, Billy felt a pang of jealousy. First she said she loved him, and she was saying she loves the whole town of Rock Creek. There seemed to be a heck of a lot he didn't know about women yet.

"Now," she continued, "about those rich snobs at the country club—and that's what they are, a bunch of rich snobs—and the reason they don't like me is because I'm the richest one of all." She hesitated. "Then if all the facts were known, I probably have more money than all the rest of them put together."

She looked at Billy. "Did you see all these tennis courts at the club?"

He nodded.

"I paid to have them put in. Did you see our big swimming pool?"

Once more he nodded.

"I paid to have that put in."

They sat there long quiet minutes, then she added, "That's why I get away with pushing myself around so much. Like telling the boat captain off and getting the rooms I wanted. I know I act like a bully once in a while, but what the heck, they're all a bunch of jerks, and they need a bully to straighten them out every now and then, and I'm just the bully that can do it." Elly threw up her hands. "That's it. Did I answer all your questions?"

Billy held up a finger. "One more."

She up and dazzled him with one of her smiles. "Shoot."

Once more Billy thought, Yep, she was just about as pretty as his Redheaded Mary.

"Well?"

He smiled back at her. "You said that you had a lot of money. Does that mean that you're one of those millionaires?"

She nodded her head "Yes."

"Where did you get all the money?"

She held up two fingers. "That's two questions."

This made them both laugh. Elly sat there for long moments with her hands folded in her lap. "I inherited it from my grandmother. She was a very wealthy woman, although I didn't know it at the time. That is while I was growing up." She looked at Billy. "You see I was raised by Grandma." She sat there for another long moment then continued, but now Elly seemed to be talking to herself.

"My father and mother never seemed to have time for me. My father with all his business ventures and golf games with his drinking buddies. My mother with her charities, her clubs, and her travels." There was a slight hesitation, and a note of sadness crept into her voice. I don't think they ever really wanted me."

Then she perked up; clapping her hands together, she said, "But my grandma did! I went to live with her when I was a very little girl. She had a huge old house that was my playpen. There were many, many rooms, and I had toys in every one of those rooms. Grandma spoiled me rotten."

Another hesitation and Elly was talking to herself again. "Grandma wasn't just my grandma. She was the one I could go to with my problems. She was the one who hugged me when I needed it. Grandma was my best friend, she was my buddy. We did everything together. Then one day she was there, and the next day she was gone. She went to bed one night, and the next morning she didn't wake up. I was devastated. I lost the most precious thing in my life, and now there will always be an empty spot in my heart.

Wow, Billy thought. *All these years I've been feeling sorry for myself because I didn't have anyone*. Why, if he had had someone real dear to him and he lost that person, he would have had to grieve the rest of his life. Nope, he sure as heck didn't want to grieve his life away. Looking at Elly, he could see how sad she was sitting there. So this time, it was him putting his arms around her and hugging her close. Elly leaned her head down on his, and they sat there in silence as the minutes ticked away. Finally, with a big sigh, Elly straightened up.

"Thank you, Billy, I needed that more than anything in the whole world. And thank you for sitting me down and giving me a good talking to, I needed that also." Elly jumped off the bed and pointed at the clock on the nightstand. "Look at the time—we're going to miss our evening meal unless we get our rears in gear."

"Get our rears in gear" made Billy laugh. He just couldn't imagine a pretty lady like Elly making statements like that. She rushed him out of the door and into the elevator. He quickly stepped forward and pushed the Down button. This was something else he would be telling the kids back at the home.

"Elevator! Oh! There's not much to them when you've been around as much as I have. Why, I can make them go up or down as easy as most people that's had years and years of experience."

Yep, he was going to have a lot of things to strut around and brag about back there.

Elly led him into a large room filled with tables and chairs. All the tables had white tablecloths and folded white napkins on them. The dining room was already filled with people, some of them already eating their food and the rest waiting to be served.

Chapter 10

Elly led him through the maze of tables to an empty one, and to Billy's amazement, there was a small plaque that said Elly Morgan.

She saw the look on his face and said, "I pay extra for this table, it belongs to me. This way I don't have to come in here and stand around waiting for someone to finish their meal so I can have a table. She snapped her fingers. "You know what, I'm going to have your name put on here along with mine."

"Yep, had my own private table, would march right on in and set down at my table and get waited on, while the other customers were standing in line waiting for an empty table. How did I manage that?" He would throw out his chest. "Well, it's knowing the right people and running with the right crowd." That would floor them.

While he was daydreaming of the glory that was to be his, Elly ordered their meal.

"Are you hungry?"

"I sure am."

"You had better be, I ordered us a huge dinner."

About that time, a waiter set a huge bowl of steaming soup in front of the two of them. Billy had noticed that all the waiters were men and each one had on a black pair of dress pants, a starched white shirt, and a black bowtie, and each one had on highly polished black shoes.

He had always thought that only ladies did this type of work. He as sure as heck would never be caught doing this sissy work.

There were plenty of crackers to go with the soup, and it was delicious. When he finished, he was getting ready to excuse himself, when the same waiter set a big dish of salad in front of him. Elly had been right—this was a big meal. At the home, when you had soup for dinner, that was it; you had soup. Billy wasn't much for salad, but this salad was covered with rich, good-tasting dressing, so he put every bite down.

He pushed back his chair.

"Elly, that was good. Now if you'll excuse me, I'll go up and watch some TV before bedtime."

Elly was staring at him with a frown on her face. "Billy, you said you were hungry."

It was his turn to frown. "I was, and like I said, it was very good." He pointed at his empty bowl and plate. "I finished, I ate every last bite."

Now a look of understanding came on her face. She placed her hand on his arm and softly said, "There's more food coming, Billy."

"Why? We've already had a good meal."

"I know, Billy, where you came from, soup and salad was a full meal. Here it's just the start of a meal. It's a different world, Billy— not a fair world but a different world." Sure enough, as she finished speaking, the same waiter appeared. He had a big round tray balanced on the palm of one hand, and he carried a small fold-up table in the other hand. Sitting the table down, he placed the tray on it.

Billy could not believe his eyes. On the tray were two large platters, and on these platters were two of the biggest steaks and baked potatoes he had ever seen. In fact, this was the first steak he had ever seen. At the home they had hamburger, and it was served in every style, shape, and form you could imagine. But steak, never, and now he had one sitting in front of him that would feed one of the boys for a week.

Once more he thought of the boys at the home. By this time of day, the evening meal was over, and each age group would be in their

BILLY YOU, NO MORE HILLS

own part of the building. There was no playing, laughing, or cutting up this time of day.

All would be quiet; best buddies would be sitting on a bunk quietly talking to each other. There would be checkers, dominos, or some other games being played, and shortly, one of the ladies would be walking through and saying "Lights out in minutes."

"Billy." Her voice brought him back to where he was. "Aren't you going to eat?"

He slowly raised his eyes and looked at her. Shaking his head, he pushed his chair back and stood up. Placing his hand on his chest, he said, "I've been thinking about my friends back there." He tapped his chest with a finger. "It just doesn't feel right in here that I have so much and they have so little."

Elly stood up and came around the table. Putting one arm around his shoulders, she gently eased him back in his chair. "I know it isn't fair, and I think it's wonderful that you care so much. But if you don't eat this steak, they're just going to throw it away. What would your buddies think of that, you wasting all this good food?"

He straightened up. By golly, Elly was right. He didn't want people going around saying that Billy had wasted good food. He glanced up. "You know it's your job to straighten me out when I'm on the wrong track, but you let a mere mortal do it for you." Then he added, "But knowing you, you will take the pay and credit for it."

Billy felt that he shouldn't add any more to it; he didn't want to go too far and get out of line.

Elly was smiling at him. "I'm not going to ask about what you said to him." She slapped the table. "Let's dig in and eat, our food is getting cold."

Cutting off a big bite of meat and placing it in his mouth, Billy bit into it. He closed his eyes; he couldn't believe that there was any food in the world that could taste this good. He let the juice run down his throat as he chewed the bite up and swallowed it.

Elly was talking. "How is your steak, Billy?"

He looked at her. "I wish I could be like a chipmunk or a squirrel. I would store some of this in my cheeks and save it for a rainy day.

Rocking back in her chair, Elly clapped her hands together and let out another one of her squeals of laughter.

Billy joined in; life was good. Still laughing, Elly said, "Billy, you are something." Billy thought to himself, Yep, he was something.

Back up in their rooms, Billy stretched. "It's been a long day, I think I'll hit the sack."

"Right after you take a shower," Elly added.

"A shower?" Billy squawked. "I took a twelve-hour bath in that old river yesterday. Besides that, at the home, we rotate our shower days."

She pointed. "To the shower, boy. This isn't the home."

Billy knew it was hopeless to argue with this lady, so he did as he was told. Drying off good, he pulled the pants of his new pajamas on, then as he was reaching across his bed to get his pajama top from where he had pitched it, he heard Elly let out a scream. He hadn't even known that she had walked into his room. Startled, he whirled around to see what the problem was.

She was on him in a flash, whirling him back around and pushing him down on the bed. He thought that she had gone crazy. Instead she was shouting at him. "Billy, who did this to you?"

He tried to push himself up and out of her grip, but she was too strong; she held him right there.

"Did what to me, what are you talking about?"

"These marks on your back, these scars."

Before he could answer her, she jerked his pajama bottoms down and was looking at his bare butt. Billy had been embarrassed a few times in his life but never like this. He could hear the boys at the home now. "She seen your naked butt. A real live woman looked at your naked rear end." Why he would be the laughingstock at the home. All the other brave stories he was going to tell about himself wouldn't mean a thing. This was the part they would remember.

"Billy, you are covered with these scars—who did this to you?"

Jerking his pajama bottoms up, he rolled over and scooted across the bed away from her. Elly slapped the bedcovers with her hand.

"Billy, you are going to tell me right now—who did this to you? Right now." There was a mean anger to her voice. He thought it best

BILLY YOU, NO MORE HILLS

to tell. He told her about the Adamses. The school, the terrible beating. The toy frog that was going to get him a worse beating. That that was why he had run away. He told her about the dogs and the windmill. The hobos, the brother-and-sister team, Martha and Delbert, and how he had dumped the chicken manure in Martha's kitchen.

The way Elly loved to laugh, he had thought the stories about the toy frog and the way that he had handled the hobos and the part about the chicken manure would put Elly on the floor rolling and screaming with laughter.

It didn't. All the while he had been telling his story, Elly had been kneeling on the floor and leaning across the bed in his direction. Her hands were gripping the bedcovers like she was ready to rip them apart. The expression on her face kind of frightened Billy. So he hurried up the part about the river and how close he came to drowning and that was all there was to it and she knew the rest of his story.

All was quiet for a moment, then Elly blurted out, "If I ever get my hands on that son of a bitch that beat you, I'll have his balls."

Billy came close to swallowing his tongue, hearing words like that coming out of a lady's mouth. He didn't think that women or girls knew about things like that. Mrs. Jamison wouldn't have enough soap handy to take care of a statement like that coming out of someone's mouth. Standing up, Elly pulled the covers over him, then darned if she didn't lean over and kiss him on the forehead. "Good night, Billy, I'll see you in the morning at breakfast time."

By *darned*, he had liked being kissed. He must be getting soft; if he wasn't careful, he would turn into one of them town-boy sissies.

The next morning, he was up early and dressed when Elly came into his room.

"Why are you up so early?"

"I need some exercise, I'm going to go out and run around the golf course."

She clapped her hands together, "Wait for me, I'll get into my sweats and run with you." Billy chuckled to himself. If this lady thought she could stay up with him running, she was in for a big surprise.

To Billy's relief, she came out in a sloppy, loose-fitting pair of sweats. He had expected her to have a pair that fit her skin tight.

Out at the edge of the golf course, they moved out at a walk, then into a slow jog. After a little of this, Billy picked up the pace. He was going to show this woman she was outclassed. Elly stayed with him; he moved out faster. She stayed with him stride for stride.

They held this pace three fourths of the way around the golf course. Then Billy kicked it into high gear. He was going to leave her far behind, eating his dust. In just a moment, she would begin to fall back. She didn't. He poured it on giving all he had. It was unbelievable; he couldn't lose this woman.

His lungs were beginning to hurt. His legs were starting to slow down; as they flashed past the end of the golf course, Elly reached out and took a hold of his arm, bringing them to a halt.

Bending over and gasping for breath, she held her side with both hands. While she was doing this, Billy doing his best to keep from showing her how bad he was winded. No way in the world did he want this young woman to know that she had run him right into the ground.

After a while, straightening up but still fighting for air, she said, "Billy, you are something!"

Without thinking about or realizing that he was doing it, Billy stepped forward and put his arms around her. "No, you are the one that's something. I didn't think there was a girl or woman in this world that could run with this boy."

Elly stepped back and, throwing her chest out, began strutting about. "Well, let me tell you something, boy. This girl in high school broke all the school records in the mile, and in college, she also won her share of races. So there, boy."

This statement sent them both into peals of laughter.

Billy thought this gal was contagious; she had him laughing as much as she laughed. "Come on, let's go swimming and cool off." Then she thought. "Oh, we didn't buy you a swimsuit, did we?"

He shook his head. "Nope."

BILLY YOU, NO MORE HILLS

"Well, the next time we go to town, we'll correct that problem. While I'm cooling off in the pool, you can cool off in the shower. How is that?"

After showering and getting dressed, Billy found Elly had already left for the pool. He couldn't go swimming, but he might as well go down and watch her enjoy the water. There was a lot of people lounging around the pool and a few in the water. Elly, dripping water, was just climbing out of the pool as Billy walked up.

He couldn't believe his eyes; she had on the skimpiest bathing suit he had ever seen. He had felt that after sitting her down and giving her that talk about things like this, she wouldn't be wearing such revealing clothes, like what she had on now.

Elly moved over to a lounge chair where she had a towel and robe draped, picking up the towel, and she began drying off. Billy quickly went over and offered her the robe.

"Here, put this on."

She gave him a puzzled look. "Why?"

"So people can't see you."

"Billy, this is a swimming pool. Everyone here has a swimsuit on."

"But the rest of them don't look naked."

Elly gave one of her little giggles. "Why thank you, Billy, you sure know how to make a girl feel good."

He threw his hands up in exasperation. Here he was, criticizing her on the way she was exposing herself, and she took it as a complement. He was going to have to be more forceful; he would hand her the robe and tell her to put it on right now. At that moment he heard a man's voice. "Good morning, Elly."

He was a tall, good-looking guy with dark hair and a narrow neat-trimmed mustache. He was dressed in a dark expensive-looking business suit with a pale blue necktie.

Elly moved over to the edge of the pool, where the man was standing. "Good morning, Ralph."

Billy took an instant dislike of the man. What right did he have coming here dressed the way he was and staring at Elly, dressed the way she was?

"How about dinner tonight?" he asked her.

She shook her head. "Not tonight."

"Why?"

"I have other plans."

"You always have other plans. Let's set a date right now, I would like to take you out."

Once more, Elly shook her head. "Ralph, like I told you before, I'm not dating anyone right now, and I'm not going to set a time or a date with you right now, but thanks for asking me."

"OK, but I don't give up easily. I'll keep pestering you until you give in."

With that, and before Elly could reply, he reached out and put his hand on her chest and gave a shove.

Elly gave out a scream as she went flying over backward into the pool.

Billy didn't hesitate or stop to think. He charged low and hard, his head hitting the good-looking man in the stomach, as his arms wrapped around the man's waist. The man went flying the same as Elly, landing flat on his back in the water, with Billy still hanging on to him. They had sunk to the bottom of the pool before Billy could break himself loose and swim to the surface and pull himself out of the water.

Ellie herself had just emerged from the pool and was staring at Billy with amazement and shock on her face.

"My god. Billy, what happened to you? How did you get in the water?"

At that moment, the man Billy had taken in with him broke the surface, spitting water and gasping for air.

Once more Elly said, "My god, what is going on here?"

Billy didn't answer. He was busy looking around for an escape route; he felt he was in deep trouble again and looked for another hill to run up.

The dapper man was not so dapper anymore and had trouble pulling himself out of the water. But finally after a slight struggle, he was standing there with water pouring from his soggy business suit; he was a sorry-looking mess.

BILLY YOU, NO MORE HILLS

All the bathers that had been lying around the pool were staring in stunned silence at the spectacle before them.

The man named Ralph, his eyes fell on Billy. "You little bastard, I'm going to wring your neck."

So saying, he headed for Billy, and Billy turned to flee, but before he could take his first steps, he heard Elly scream, "You will do no such thing!" She grabbed hold of Billy, pulling him to her. He had felt a lot of embarrassment in his life lately but nothing like this. One of her hands was on the back of his head, holding him tight to her with his face buried between her upper naked bosom. What a spot for a twelve-year-old boy to be in with the whole wide world watching. He tried pushing himself free, but the only purchess hold his hand could find was naked body. He jerked his hand back as if he had touched hot coals. He stood there helplessly; his face was at that place and his arms hanging at his side as Elly and Ralph were shouting at each other.

This was another one of his adventures the boys at the home wouldn't hear about. Oh, he would brag about tackling this guy and taking him to the bottom of the pool, but the part that was happening now—no way. They would go wild over this one. "You actually had your fish between a woman's real live naked breasts." Yep. This is one he would keep to himself.

Now Elly pushed him back with a hand on each side of his face. She bent over to him nose to nose. "Billy, why did you do this?"

This was the first time he had ever seen anger on her face and in her eyes.

His answer—"I thought he had hurt you."

Her voice softened. "You thought he hurt me?"

"When I heard you scream, I thought he had hurt you bad, and I'm never going to let anyone hurt you."

Her face softened, and her smile was back. Then to his disgust, she placed his face right back between those two things. And Elly and Ralph were shouting at each other again. Finally after what seemed like forever, it was over, and Ralph was stomping off in anger in one direction, and she was leading him off in another. To his relief, she picked up her robe and put it on.

He was soaking wet, and every step he took his shoes made a loud squishing sound. Up the pathway they went and into the lobby—*squish, squish, squish.*

All the lounge lizards, as Billy called them, stopped what they were doing and jerked to attention as they heard this strange sound coming at them.

There were three young men by the counter. They also stopped what they were doing or talking about and looked to see what the strange squishing sound was all about.

Then to Billy's utter horror and amazement, Elly took her robe off, right in front of those men, which caused their mouths to drop open and freeze them in place.

She draped the robe around him. "Here, Billy, put this on before you catch your death of cold." In Billy's mind's eye she was practically bare butt naked as she led him into the elevator.

When the elevator doors closed, she began jumping up and down, clapping her hands together and laughing her fool head off. "Boy, I sure knocked those guys' eyes out, didn't I?"

Once more he was laughing with her. He might as well give up; there was no way in the world he was going to change this young lady. She had fun with everything she did. He was going to accept that and have fun right along with her.

That evening, they had another big fine meal at their private table.

The next morning after breakfast, Elly began rushing about. "Billy, I've got to run into town and take care of some banking business, then I'm going to get my hair fixed. I'll be back in time for lunch, then you and I will go for a nice drive. How does that sound?"

"Fine!" he told her.

Then she was gone, rushing out the door in a hurry; everything this woman did seemed to be in a rush of energy.

He went out and took a slow jog around the golf course then went down by the river. It was a nice, beautiful day. He sat down and leaned back against a rock and watched the water flow by. For the first time in his life, Billy felt at peace with the world.

BILLY YOU, NO MORE HILLS

"You are probably floating around on a soft cloud up there, taking credit for what's been happening to me lately. Well, let me tell you, I'm in a good mood today, so I'll throw some of the credit your way. But this young lady, Elly, she is the one who has turned it all around for me. Of course I can hear you right now, telling some of those angels fluttering around up there, waiting on you hand and foot, 'Well, who does that boy think it was that sent Elly to him, or him to her—whatever?'"

Billy laughed to himself. It had been a while since he had had this long a chat with the old boy up there. Life was good.

Time skipped past; it was about time for lunch to be served.

Standing up and stretching, he jogged back up to the country club and around to the car parking lot. Elly's little red sports car wasn't there yet.

Inside, people were already moving into the dining room; it was lunchtime. He paced the lounge floor, going to the door at times, looking out at the parking lot—still no Elly. Well, he was hungry. She would just have to have lunch by herself when she got here.

He went into the dining room and swaggered over to his private table; he was really enjoying this.

After lunch, he moved back out in the lobby. He guessed he would go up and watch a little television.

There was a group of people standing by the counter talking excitedly with the clerk. As Billy moved into the stairwell, which lately he had been using instead of the elevator, he heard a high, screechy voice coming out of the group at the counter. "The wild way she drove that little car, we all knew it bound to happen sooner or later."

Billy caught his breath; he knew who the lady had to be talking about.

He eased back to the entrance way of the stairwell where he could see but not be seen. Another voice came from the gathering. "What time did this happen?"

"Well, she left here early this morning, but it wasn't until about an hour ago that a fisherman found her wrecked car in the bottom of the creek bed."

Billy staggered back and sat down on the bottom step; he was having trouble breathing.

"How bad was it?" a voice asked.

The person that seemed to know all the details answered, "It couldn't be worse. Her car is a twisted wreck of metal. You can't even tell it was a car, and the young lady Miss Morgan—well, she was torn up real bad. They said just about every bone in her body was broken, and she wasn't breathing when they brought her up."

Billy didn't wait to hear any more. He went stumbling up the stairs to their rooms, where he fell on his bed in a state of shock. This couldn't be true; this could not have happened to Elly.

He didn't lie there long; he had to get into town and see for himself how bad Elly really was.

The lady down at the counter had to be mistaken; Elly was too tough for it to be as bad as the lady made it sound. He would probably find her bruised and banged up some, and when he found her, she would hit him with one of her giggles and make some silly remark about what happened. But inside of himself, he knew that it was bad, and he couldn't imagine his life without her.

He hesitated before going out the door; he had better go prepared. Going to the bed, he jerked the thick comforter back and threw it aside.

The blanket underneath, he rolled into a bedroll. Looking about, all he could see to make a sling out of was the window drape cord. He didn't hesitate; quickly removing it, he had the cord around the blanket and the blanket slung across his back.

He had to be careful. Elly wasn't here to protect him.

He was on his own again. Cautiously opening the door, he looked out; the hallway was vacant. He sprinted down it to the back stairway he had found on one of his exploring trips. At the bottom of the stairs, there was a door leading out into the back parking lot. He went through the lot at a run. Through it, he veered off to the left, aiming for the road that would take him into Rock Creek and to Elly.

It was downhill, so he was making good time.

Occasionally he would hear a car, and he would duck behind a rock or bush until it passed.

Chapter 11

The sun was dropping fast, and this was good. He didn't want to be caught walking Rock Creek streets in the daylight with a bedroll slung across his back. He didn't have to worry; it was full dark by the time he reached the outskirts of town. And like most small towns or villages, activity stopped, stores closed their doors, and people moved in doors to their dinner tables or parked themselves in front of their televisions.

Staying in the shadows as much as he could, Billy moved quietly through the streets. He had noted when he had come to Rock Creek with Elly that the hospital sat diagonally across the street from the café that they had eaten lunch in. Then it entered his head that the police station was on the opposite side of the street from the café.

He approached that intersection with caution. The café was still open, and there were three or four customers inside eating their evening meals.

Lights were on in the police station, but he could not see anyone moving about. Cautiously moving across the street to the hospital entrance, he hesitated; it wouldn't be wise to take his bedroll inside. There were three steps leading up to a deck, which had handrails around it and a canopy over it, that you had to go up and across to reach the door way to the building. There was crawl space underneath the deck, and this is where Billy placed his bedroll. Then taking a deep nervous breath, he went up the steps and into the hos-

CLARENCE W. LESLIE

pital. Inside there was a long well-lit hallway with a nurses desk about halfway down.

There was a lady nurse sitting at the desk doing some paperwork. She was the only person in sight.

As Billy approached the desk, he passed a hallway running left and right from the main hallway; they were not as long or as well-lit. The lady kept on typing as Billy stopped in front of the desk. He waited a moment then spoke; the nurse gave a startled jerk.

"Oh, I'm sorry, I didn't see you come in. How can I help you?"

Billy cleared his throat and hesitantly said, "I came to see how Miss Elly Morgan is doing," then he added, "and I would like to visit with her if I may."

The nurse gave him a long look. "Are you related to Miss Morgan?"

He hesitated a moment, not really knowing how to answer that, then he recalled Elly telling the boat captain and the desk clerk that he, Billy, was her brother.

"I'm her brother."

Now it was the nurse's turn to hesitate. "I didn't know Elly had a brother." Now the nurse had a sad expression on her face. "I think it would be best if you talked to the doctor."

She pushed a button and spoke into a mike. "Dr. Pepper, could you come to the front desk, please?" Then looking at Billy and still in a soft voice she said, "The doctor will be here shortly. If you care to sit, there are some chairs by the wall."

He didn't care to sit. He paced the hallway, nervous and scared, hoping and praying the doctor would bring good news about Elly. The front door from the outside came flying open, and a tall, well-dressed, distinguished-looking man came charging in. Right on his heels was a woman just as well-dressed and distinguished-looking as the man. They brushed past Billy without looking at him, as though he didn't exist. He could feel power coming from this pair, and he knew who they were before the man spoke.

"My name is Ralph Morgan. My wife and I have come to check on the condition of our daughter."

BILLY YOU, NO MORE HILLS

Billy could hear the nervousness in the nurse's voice; she must have felt the power in these people also.

"Mr. Morgan, Dr. Pepper will be here in a moment." Elly's father slapped the nurses desk with his open hand. "I didn't come here to see a doctor, I came to see Elly. What room is she in?"

"Sir, I'm sorry, but you will have to wait for the doctor.""Nurse, do you know who I am?"

"Yes, Mr. Morgan, I know who you are, but I do not have the authority to give out information."

Billy gained respect for this nurse; though she was intimidated, she was standing up to this bullying man.

As for Billy, he had taken an instant dislike to Elly's parents.

"Nurse, I do not have time to play games with you. Take us to our daughter right now or I will see to it that you are removed from your position by the end of this day." The nurse put her hands on her hips and took a step toward Mr. Morgan. Billy thought, *Good, she is going to give this obnoxious man a good tongue lashing,* but just as she was opening her mouth to speak, a tall grey-haired man came out of a door close by. He had on a pale-green pullover blouse and matching green pull-on pants. He even had green booties covering his shoes.

"Mr. and Mrs. Morgan, I'm glad you are here."

"How is Elly?"

The doctor shook his head. "If you will come with me, you will have a few minutes to tell her good-bye, but I must warn you, it won't be a pretty sight. She is badly banged up. Also, she is in a coma and won't recognize you. I'm terribly, terribly sorry—there is no way she will last through the hour."

This last statement made Billy's knees buckle, and it felt as if his heart had stopped beating. He backed all the way down the hall to the door, and as he stepped outside, a bright flash of lightning went streaking across the sky, followed by a roll of thunder, and as Billy crawled underneath the porch, big raindrops came pelting down, and the boy that had never cried for himself opened up his heart and let the tears flow for the terrible loss that he felt.

The rain came down and lasted most of the night, but Billy didn't hear it; all he could think about was Elly. The w y she laughed and giggled, the way she teased people, the fun she had with life. But most of all the way he and she had hit it off, right from the beginning. She had taken him in under her wing and showed him the good side of life. Now that was all gone, he felt that he was on the run again, with nowhere to go. These thoughts kept traveling through his mind long after the rain had stopped and light was breaking in the east. But finally he fell into a deep exhausted sleep. Footsteps on the floor above him, along with talk and laughter, woke him up. He lay there startled for long moments, wondering what was happening and where he was at. Then the events of yesterday filtered back in, and once more sadness engulfed him. But he knew that he didn't have time to dwell on it; he had to get moving. His stomach was growling with hunger pains as he rolled up his bedroll.

Crawling to the edge of the porch, he looked out and was startled to see how high the sun was. He had really overslept; he should have been up and on his way by sun up.

Moving from underneath his shelter, he stood up and stretched. The morning was bright and fresh from the rain the night before. It was going to be a nice day for a walk. Slinging his bedroll across his back, he crossed the street and was walking past the front of the bank building when out of the corner of his eye, he saw a police car pull up to the curb by the police station. His heart gave a small skip or two as he picked up his pace. He eased his bedroll off his back and tucked it under his arm, hoping he would look more like a kid carrying a package than a runaway kid with his bedroll on his back. He felt that he was going to get away with it, then one of the officers called out, "Hey, boy, hold up a minute."

Billy thought fast; he turned and waved at the police officers as if he hadn't understood what they had said.

"Good morning, officers, it's a beautiful day, isn't it?" He increased his pace; every step he gained would be in his favor. He felt another foot race coming on.

One of the policemen stepped off the curb. He was young-looking, and he was tall and slim. Billy knew this was going to be his greatest challenge yet.

BILLY YOU, NO MORE HILLS

"Just a moment, son, we would like to talk to you." Billy waved and smiled at them again as if he still didn't understand what was being said.

The young policeman took a couple of steps into the street. "Come back here, boy, right now." Billy slung his bedroll back across his back; he would need both his arms for pumping action when he started to run.

Up ahead of him at the end of the block, he could see a park with trees and green grass. There were kids' swings and a playground and barbecue pits, but most of all—and this made Billy hopes soar— about halfway across the park, the ground began to rise, and then it became very steep. It was still covered with grass and trees, but once more, he had his hill. He glanced heaven ward. "Thanks!"

It was time; he began his run. There was a startled shout from behind. "Hey!"

Billy took a quick look over his shoulder. The young officer had jumped out into the street and was running right down the middle of that street, and he was moving fast. Billy's hill was still a long way off; he hoped and prayed that he could reach it before the policeman caught up with him. Reaching the end of the block, he darted out into the cross street. He didn't see the car until he heard the squeal of the brakes and the angry blaring of the horn. It didn't slow him down, but it did the young cop, who had to come to a screeching halt as the upset driver gunned his car down the road. This gave Billy a few precious steps as he hurdled the low fence that went around the park.

The start of the hill was just a few heartbeats away, but the policeman was just a few heartbeats away from stepping on his heels.

Billy hit the bottom slope of the hill at a flat dead run. He gave a sigh of relief; the hill was much steeper up close than it had looked from the spot where he had begun his mad dash. The cop was practicality breathing down his neck. "Stop, son, just want to talk to you."

Billy could hear a shortness of breath in the man's voice, which gave Billy more energy and speed to his flying feet. They were on the steepest part of the hill now, and though he couldn't see behind him, Billy could feel the man falling back a step or two. "Yep," Billy chor-

CLARENCE W. LESLIE

tled to himself; he could run uphill faster than most people could run downhill.

Now he felt he had the luxury of looking back; sure enough the young man was fading fast. A big smile lit up Billy's face as he went flying on up the hill, then the smile left as fast as it had come. Billy had crested out the top of the hill. Before him was a long, wide sloping plateau covered with green grass and huge beautiful homes spotted here and there, and they all seemed to have white picket fences around them. Far to his right was the steep winding road going up to the country club. It was much too far away, even for a runner like himself, to reach before someone caught up with him. Moments back he had felt so gleeful that once more he had outrun his pursuer. Now a hopelessness closed in around him. Where was he running to anyway? He had no idea where the home was; he was lost. He heaved another big sigh, this time of resignation. Slowly turning, he moved back down the hill to where the young cop was sitting and watching him.

He eased down beside the man. They both sat there for long moments, neither saying a word. The cop was still breathing a little heavily. Billy spoke first. "You should quit smoking." The cop looked at him, then reaching into his shirt pocket, he pulled out a pack of cigarettes and pitched them away. "Why did you run?"

Billy took a deep breath before answering, "I've been running all my life, that's all I know how to do."

"Why did you stop?" the officer asked with a puzzled sound to his voice. The officer didn't think the young boy was ever going to answer him, and when he did, the boy seemed to be talking to himself and in a soft voice hardly above a whisper. "I don't have any more hills to run up."

The officer didn't understand the meaning of the statement, but he knew that it meant something to the boy. "Where are your parents, son?"

"I don't have any parents. I've never had any parents. I'm an orphan."

The officer understood that this dejected young boy sitting beside him had problems, more problems than kids this age should

BILLY YOU, NO MORE HILLS

have. He gently placed his hand on the boy's shoulder. "What's your name?"

"Billy."

"What's your last name?"

Billy shook his head. "I don't have a last name, and the name Billy is just borrowed. It doesn't really belong to me."

All of a sudden, Billy realized he was sitting here feeling sorry for himself, trying to get sympathy from this nice young cop. He jumped up. "I'm ready to go if you are."

They walked back down the hill, through the park and up the street to where the other cop was waiting for them.

He asked, "What kind of problems do we have here, Tom?"

Tom laughed. "The only problem I have is that for the first time in my life, I lost a foot race. This young man here—his name is Billy—has a few problems, and we are going to give him a hand and help him solve them. Come on, let's go inside the police station."

It was one large room as far as Billy could tell, with three desks lined up along the far wall, and across the room from the desks, there were three prison cells. Billy had never seen a prison cell, but he knew that this is what they had to be.

All three of the small rooms had metal bars in front of them. Sitting behind the middle desk sat an older man; he was wearing a business suit with a white shirt and tie.

"Tom!" he barked out. "When you capture a dangerous criminal, the rules are you bring him in here with handcuffs on and a gun at his head. Do you understand me?"

Upon saying this, the older man winked at Billy. The man behind the desk continued, "What's the matter, Tom, what kind of problems do we have here?"

"Nothing serious, Chief. All we have, I believe, is a young man that needs a helping hand."

The chief looked at Billy. "That's what we're here for, son, to give a people a helping hand when they need it. Tell me your problem, and I will do everything we can to help solve it."

Billy didn't go in to a lot of detail. He told about being sent to a foster home and that Mr. and Mrs. Adams, the foster parents, had treated him real good. Then he told about the beating the principal had given him and that he felt he was about to get another one and didn't think he could take it, so he had run away and was trying to get back to the Mayhill Boys' Home.

All was quiet for a while, then the chief spoke. "I know where the boys' home is. And I know Mrs. Jamison. I'll give her a call and have her send over some transportation to get you back there. How's that?"

The chief continued, "We'll fix up one of our cells there, where you will have a nice warm bed to spend the night. How does that sound?"

Once more Billy nodded his head; it sure as heck sounded good to him.

Then he had to ask the question that had been on his mind ever since Elly had had her car wreck. "Sir, there was a young lady that had a car wreck yesterday. I wonder—how is she doing?"

The chief looked at him with a question in his eyes. "You know Elly?"

Billy felt it best not to go into a lot of detail. "I have met her, sir, that's about it."

The older man sadly shook his head. "What a terrible shame, I've known that girl all her life. One of the nicest young ladies that ever was." There was a long pause. "She's sure going to be missed around here."

The two young officers solemnly agreed.

Billy fought back the tears welling in his eyes; he didn't want these men to see how deep his hurt was.

Tom placed a hand on Billy's shoulder. "When's the last time you ate, son?"

Billy thought about it and realized it had been a while. "Lunch yesterday, sir."

"Wow, you must be starved. I tell you what, my wife works in the café across the street there. You go on over there and tell her to fix you up a big hamburger, some French fries, and a shake and tell her to put it on my tab."

Billy wanted to ask him what the heck a tab was.

BILLY YOU, NO MORE HILLS

But he was too hungry to wait for an answer on it. He said. "Yes, sir." As he was going out the door, he stopped and stuck his head back in the door. "Sir, how will I know your wife?"

"That's easy, Billy, she's the prettiest lady in there."

Billy nodded his head in understanding as he headed for the cafe. But once inside the café, he pulled up short. There were three waitresses working, and to a twelve-year-old boy they all looked pretty—of course not as pretty as Elly or Redheaded Mary, but each one of them pretty enough to confuse him in which one to pick as Officer Tom's wife.

There was not many customers in the place, this time of day. There was an older man and woman sitting in a front booth by the window and two that looked like working men sitting in one of the back booths drinking coffee. There was no one sitting at the counter, so this is where Billy moved to and sat down at an end stool. And all the while, he was studying the three ladies. Two of them were tall, slim-built and blond-headed, both pretty in Billy's estimation; the third one was smaller and, to Billy, kinda dainty looking. She had really black short hair and was darker complexioned than the two blondes and she had very black (to him what seemed like) laughing eyes.

This was the one he picked. As he sat down, one of the blond ladies moved over and asked, "Yes, sir, may I help you?" He thought it odd that she called him sir, but that was probably just her way of being friendly.

He answered. "Yes, ma'am, I need to talk to that lady." So saying, he pointed to the dark-headed woman at the far end of the counter. The blonde in front of him called out, "Hey, Sadie, there's a handsome young gentleman here that wants to talk to you."

This caused Billy to straighten up and throw out his chest a mite. Even older grown-up women noted that he was a handsome, good-looking boy.

The lady named Sadie was standing in front of him. "May I help you?"

"Yes, ma'am, your husband, Officer Tom, sent me here. He said he would pay for me a hamburger, fries, and chocolate shake.

"He did, did he?"

"Yes, ma'am."

"He's always doing this to me." In midstride, he turned back to him. "Just how did you know that I was Tom's wife?"

Billy knew the second that he answered her question, the way he did that it was a mistake. "Your husband said that you would be the prettiest lady here."

She straightened up with a surprised look on her face, then a big smile replaced the surprised look, then she clapped her hands together for attention.

"Girls, come down here, there's something I want you to hear." Billy looked back over his shoulder at the door. If he wasn't so hungry, he would escape this place and the three ladies now standing in front of him.

Sadie placed her hand on his, which was resting on the counter. He wanted to jerk his hand away but felt it would be rude, so he sat there with him and this lady practically holding hands, or so he thought.

"What's your name?"

"Billy, ma'am."

"Now, Billy, I want you to tell these two ladies how you recognized me. Tell them exactly as you told me."

Sadie tapped her foot with a smirk on her face as she waited for his answer.

God, why did women always want to be told they were pretty? he thought as he racked his brain, trying to come up with the right answer to make all three women happy. This was a delicate situation.

He was going to have to up and tell them what he felt they wanted to hear, and that was that. That they were all pretty but at the same time giving Sadie the edge.

He took a deep breath; he hoped that he could pull this off.

"Officer Tom told me to come to the cafe here and that his wife would fix me a hamburger, fries, and a chocolate shake. He said the way I would know his wife is that she was the prettiest lady here."

Sadie clapped her hands again. "That's it, girls, now we know. Back to work."

BILLY YOU, NO MORE HILLS

He blurted out, "It was hard, real hard, you are all three real pretty."

That brought laughter from the three. "Where's your parents?"

He told them that he was an orphan trying to make it back to the Mayhill Boys' Home where he belonged.

Questions came pouring in. So he began telling them about the harrowing and terrifying adventures he had been through. Boy, he had their attention now; all three were leaning across the counter, oohing and aahing at every word he uttered.

Now one of the ladies was holding his other hand, squeezing it tight—no doubt about it, this boy really had it.

Here he was sitting at the counter in a café, holding hands with two pretty women. Billy was bragging about all the trouble he had been through and the way he had handled them, but he didn't want these ladies to know that, so he kept his voice sad and humble, just a poor orphan boy fighting his way through life the best way he knew how.

No telling how long this would have gone on if the cook hadn't slammed a plate with the hamburger and fries down on the counter and at the same time saying, "You have more than one customer in here, ladies."

The cook went back to the kitchen. The three ladies went back to doing what waitresses do. Billy ate his meal in peace.

Back at the police station, the chief told Billy to make himself at home, which Billy did.

He wandered in and out of the three empty cells, reading the wanted flyers on the bulletin board, until at last he became bored. Going into the middle cell, he stretched out on the cot that was in there, and in a very short period of time, he was sound asleep.

Chapter 12

The chief tugging on the toe of his shoe brought Billy into a startled state of awakeness, wondering where he was at and ready to flee. The gentle voice of the police chief said, "Easy, boy, easy, boy!"

That brought Billy back to reality and to realizing where he was. Pointing to a small table, which was bolted to the wall of the cell and upon which sat a food tray, the chief said, "Here's you a nice evening meal, enjoy it. I'm calling it a day. There will be a night watchman in and out during the night. Just ignore him and get yourself a good night's sleep, and in the morning, we will have you on your way home. Good night, son."

After his meal, Billy flopped back down on the cot and slept the night away.

The next morning, Officer Tom took him across the street to the café, where the two of them had a big breakfast. Upon leaving the café, Billy could see the Mayhill van sitting in front of the police station. Billy knew who the driver would be. It was Silent Jake, as the boys called him. His name was Jake Turner. A dour-looking old man that rarely spoke a word, hence the name Silent Jake.

After a few good-byes and thanks, Billy got into one of the backseats of the van. He knew that's what Silent Jake preferred. Jake seemed to like having Mrs. Jamison ride up front with him, but if anyone else sat up there, he seemed to get sourer and grayer looking, never saying a word, no matter how long the ride.

BILLY YOU, NO MORE HILLS

Billy was surprised at how close he had come to making it back here on his own. He had been so lost but yet so close to the boys' home. If he had made it across that wide river, he would have been here in a few short days' time.

Now he felt apprehensive about with the thought of facing Mrs. Jamison. Silent Jake pulled in front of the big front door and discharged his passenger and went wheeling away. There in front of Billy were the steps he had conquered while leaving with Mr. and Mrs. Adams. To Billy it seemed like it had been another lifetime away, but looking back, it hadn't been all that long.

Easing up the steps and through the door, there she was, hands on hips, waiting for him, but now, to Billy, she didn't seem nearly as tall, and she appeared to be somewhat older.

"Well, well, the wandering boy has returned." She stood there waiting for his answer; he had none except "Yes, ma'am."

"Where are your other clothes, and where did you get those?" So saying, she pointed to the ones he had on.

"I lost the ones I took with me. A nice lady, a very nice lady, bought these for me." That was all the answer she was going to get. Mrs. Jamison seemed to realize that and with hands still on her hips, she went, "Ump."

Then she turned and walked away saying, "Follow me."

This insulted Billy. She didn't have to lead him to where she wanted him to go. He knew the ins and outs of this huge building as well as she did. All she had to do was tell him where she wanted him to go. But no, she had to lead him along like he was a little kid that didn't know how to find his way. As they left the office complex and entered a long wide hallway, doors came flying open, and kids came streaming out of these doors, headed for lunch break. Some of the boys stopped to stare for a moment. Some envied him, and some of the smaller boys came running to him saying, "Billy, Billy, you're back."

Mrs. Jamison would have none of this and shushed them on their way. Yep, he was back and glad to be here.

She led him into the bunk room for boys his age and, pointing, said, "The top bunk on the far end is not being used. That one will be yours."

Turning, she began marching for the exit.

Billy did not want to be in this room that would be full of sleeping boys each night. "Mrs. Jamison."

She stopped but did not turn around. "Yes?"

"Can I have my cot back in the hallway? Please." For long moments he didn't think she was going to answer him.

"That's up to you." With that, she was gone. So was he; he found the cot and bedding where he had left it. He was back where he belonged.

In a few short days, he was back in the everyday routine of the home. But he himself had changed. He didn't go around with a chip on his shoulder like he had in the past.

He did go back to studying at night after lights out and the other boys had settled in for a night's sleep. In the classroom, he did not hold up his test papers to show all the other boys the As he received.

He did not do anything to upset or antagonize the teachers.

All the stories he was going to tell about his adventures on the long road home and all the bragging he was going to do, he told no one but Mrs. Jamison, and there was no bragging in it nor asking for sympathy.

He asked for an audience with her, which she granted. He sat down in her office; it was a Sunday afternoon.

In a very quiet voice, he explained to her why he had run away from the foster home and the school. He didn't go into a lot of detail on the problems he had getting back, but he did touch on all the highlights so she would understand and appreciate what he had been through. In all his telling, she sat with folded hands behind her desk, never interrupting him. As his story ended, they both sat for long moments, not speaking.

At the door, he turned back to her and said, "Thank you, ma'am, for listening to me."

BILLY YOU, NO MORE HILLS

As he opened the door and started out, she spoke in the softest voice he had ever heard her use, "Thank you, Billy, for telling me."

A few days later, she sent word that she would like to see Billy in her office.

He wondered what the heck he had done now to upset her.

At Mrs. Jamison's door, he gave a soft rap.

"Come in, Billy."

He went in not knowing what to expect, and not knowing what to expect, he went in with a chip on his shoulder. He had been in this office many times, probably more than any one other boy that had lived here at the home. And most of the time it had been for a chewing out, which she thought he had coming and for which he felt he didn't have coming.

He remembered on one occasion she had called him a big bully for picking on the other kids. This had really upset Billy. He had always thought of a bully as someone that beat up kids smaller than themselves. Billy had never done that. Sure, every so often he would punch one of the boys, but always the ones his age or a little older. And he never punched anyone out unless they had it coming.

"Sit down, Billy."

The way she said, "Sit down, Billy" caught him off guard. In the past, her words to him always seemed to come in the form of an order.

Today it seemed as if Mrs. Jamison was asking him to sit.

He sat with hands folded in his lap, waiting for her to speak.

Mrs. Jamison sat as if in deep thought for a moment then. "Billy, it seems to me that Mr. Cook hasn't been feeling too well lately. Doesn't it appear that way to you?"

He was nodding his head yes before she had finished speaking. And at the same time, amazed that she was asking his opinion. "Yes, ma'am, I've noticed that two or three times in the last two days. I've seen him stagger and grab something to hold on to, as if he were real dizzy or something." Now Mrs. Jamison nodded her head. "I've noticed the same thing." Then she added, "I've talked to Mr. Cook and told him that I wanted to let him have some of the boys to help him. She paused. "Guess what?"

"What?"

"He asked for you."

Billy sat up straight and wide-eyed and, in amazement, said, "He did?"

"Yes, he did."

The way she said this left Billy with the impression that she couldn't believe Mr. Cook had asked for him. She continued, "For the time being, Mr. Cook said all the help he needs will be at breakfast time."

Mrs. Jamison paused, and Billy waited, knowing there was more to come. Placing her folded hands on her desk and leaning forward, in a stern voice, she told him, "You will have to get up somewhat earlier than you have been, and for you to get to classes on time, you will have to finish up the chores Mr. Cook gives you as fast as you possibly can. Do you think you can handle it?" Mrs. Jamison stood up, and Billy knew that this was her way of telling him that he was dismissed. As he opened the door to leave, she surprised him by stating. "Mr. Cook will be the only chores you have for the time being."

All he could say was, "Thank you, ma'am!"

Mr. Cook had a spare alarm clock that he loaned Billy and informed him that for the time being, breakfast was all he would need Billy to help him with. He told Billy that it was getting more and more difficult to get up and get going in the mornings.

Billy found it easy to fall into the routine of getting breakfast prepared for the group of hungry boys each morning. There was a set menu for each morning; in fact, there was a set menu for each and every day. Without fail, that was what was placed on the tables.

As the days slipped by, Billy became more and more concerned and worried about old Mr. Cook. He had always been so spry and active, but now it seemed as if he were going downhill fast. Each morning he would come out of his room, which was located right off the kitchen, later and later. It had reached the point where Billy would have Mr. Cook's coffee really when he came out of his room. There was a small table in the kitchen with only two chairs. This is where Mr. Cook would head to, and by the time he had sat down, Billy would have a cup of coffee poured and sitting in front of him.

BILLY YOU, NO MORE HILLS

The cook would always have something nice to say in thanks for the coffee being ready, like "Thanks, Billy," or "What in hell would I do without you, boy?" or some other words along these lines.

The first thing Billy did as he went into the kitchen each morning was to turn the huge grill on so it would start heating up. Then he would put Mr. Cook's coffee on to boil. The cook had an old-fashioned granite coffeepot he made his coffee in, the old-fashioned way.

Then he would get all the ingredients out for the meal they would make for that day. By the time the grill was hot and the coffee was ready, Mr. Cook would come out of his room.

On Saturdays, Sundays, or holidays, there wasn't quite the rush to get the food ready. The boys were given a little more time to enjoy their food on these days.

It was a Sunday morning. Billy was in the kitchen early as usual. The grill was hot, the coffee made, and still no Mr. Cook. Pancakes and bacon was the Sunday morning menu. Billy got the pancake mix out and mixed two large bowls of it. It took that much for this large group of boys.

When the cook still hadn't made his appearance, Billy knew that they were running out of time. He opened up the packages of bacon and put some on to cook on one half of the grill; the other half would be used for the pancakes.

Each boy got two of these huge pancakes and four slices of bacon. This was the favorite meal for most of the kids.

Still no cook. Billy was getting nervous and worried; it was getting close to feeding time. Hurriedly he went over to Mr. Cook's bedroom door and timidly knocked on it. There was no answer. He knocked again, this time louder, and called out, "Mr. Cook?"

Still no answer. Taking a hold of the doorknob, Billy opened the door wide enough for him to look in. It was a small but very neat room, but with not too much furniture in it. There was one large recliner chair with an end table sitting right next to it. Across the room was a television set. And hanging on the walls were six or seven pictures of ships. Billy assumed they were some of the ships the cook had worked on. Across the room there was an open door leading into a small bathroom. Pushing the door open wider and stepping into

CLARENCE W. LESLIE

the room, Billy called out, "Mr. Cook." There was no answer, but now he could see the old cook lying on his bed or, rather, a cot not much bigger than the one Billy slept on in the hallway.

"Mr. Cook, it's time to start feeding the boys" Still no response.

Billy tentatively stepped forward and placed his hand on Mr. Cook's leg and gave it a slight shake. "Mr. Cook?"

The cook's body was completely rigid. Then Billy remembered reading or hearing that when a person died, they did it with their eyes wide open.

Letting out a frightened yelp, Billy bolted from the room. He didn't stop running until he was out of the kitchen and into the mess hall, where the boys were beginning to gather for their breakfast.

Billy stood there taking deep breaths as he fought his panic attack. "Oh, my gosh," he said to himself. Someone had to do the cooking, and he knew that someone was him.

Going back into the kitchen, he sided over to the cook's bedroom door and closed it. This made him feel better about the dead body lying so close by.

Then it hit him that he had touched Mr. Cook's dead body. Rushing over to the big kitchen sink, he ran scalding hot water over his hands. He sure didn't want to catch whatever it was the cook had died from.

The first batch of bacon was done. Scooping it up, he placed it in a strainer and put more on the grill. The grill was huge, and on the other half of it, he poured on twelve large pancakes. By the time these were cooked, boys were there holding out their platters to be filled. It was a hectic half hour, so Billy put everything out of his mind and concentrated on the job at hand. When the last of the boys walked out of the kitchen with food in hand, he heaved a huge sigh of relief, and he felt proud of himself. He had cooked a complete meal for the large group of boys and had not made one mistake. It was time to cook his own meal now.

Turning around, he let out a startled gasp and took a step back. With arms folded across her chest, Mrs. Jamison was standing just inside the door on the opposite side of the room that the boys had been going in and out of. This door led out into the business part of

BILLY YOU, NO MORE HILLS

the building, where the offices, classrooms, and such were located. She was the first to speak. "Where's Mr. Cook?"

Billy decided that he was going to play this very casual, even though his heart was still racing a mile a minute. Mrs. Jamison came in at this time each morning, and she and the cook would sit down at the small table over against the wall and have a cup of coffee and do some visiting while going over some of the day's business.

Pouring a cup full of coffee, he sat it on the table for her before he answered, "He's no longer with us, ma'am."

"What do you mean 'he's no longer with us.'"

"He's dead, ma'am."

There was a startled "What?" Billy pointed at the closed door leading into the cook's room.

"He went to sleep last night and just didn't wake up this morning, ma'am."

Mrs. Jamison stared at Billy for long moments as if not knowing whether to believe him or not. Then striding over to the closed door, she opened it and stepped into the room where Mr. Cook's dead body lay in the bed. Billy didn't follow her into the room; never again did he want to set foot in there.

It seemed to Billy that Mrs. Jamison was in there a long time before she finally came out. He didn't know why he thought it, but he felt even though there were no tears in her eyes that Mrs. Jamison had been crying.

Sitting down at the table, she stared at her cup of coffee long, long moments before taking a sip of it. Looking at Billy, she almost whispered, "Please join me."

Billy had tried coffee a time or two and didn't really like it, but now he poured himself a cup and sat down across from the head lady.

They sat there sipping their coffee, neither talking. Mrs. Jamison finished her coffee and went and refilled it. Sitting back down at the table, she spoke. "Billy, you fixed breakfast and served it all by yourself, didn't you?"

"Yes, ma'am."

Then to Billy's surprise and amazement, she placed her hand on his and squeezed it. This caught Billy so far off guard he just about jerked his hand free and bolted from the room, but he didn't.

"Finding Mr. Cook the way you did, it must have been a terrible shock."

He nodded his head.

She continued, "I don't know how to thank you for getting the boys' breakfast ready." Then Mrs. Jamison threw her hands up in the air. "Speaking of the boys, I'll have to tell them that while they are still in the mess hall."As Mrs. Jamison stood up to do this, Billy's teacher and the home nurse came in the kitchen for their cup of coffee. Now these two ladies didn't come in for coffee each and every morning the way Mrs. Jamison did. But they did come in quite often, and they always had a short visit with Mr. Cook.

Mrs. Jamison went up close to the two women and, in a very soft voice, told them about the cook's death and how Billy was the one that had found him. They both looked at Billy with shock on their eyes, and his schoolteacher rushed to him and put her arms around him in a tight hug, and there were tears in her eyes. He didn't know if it was for him or the dead cook.

Then as she stepped back, the nurse had her arms around him, pulling him up too close and rocking him back and forth like you would a baby or maybe a girl but not a boy his age. Those were Billy's thoughts.

When they were through hugging him and patting him with their hands and telling him how sorry they were that it was he, Billy, that had found the dead cook, the three ladies, as a group, went into where the rest of the boys were eating their breakfast to tell them of Mr. Cook's passing.

Taking a bunch of deep rapid breaths to shore up his nerve, Billy went back into the cook's room. Looking down at the dead man where he lay on his bed, Billy saw that his eyes were closed, and he knew that Mrs. Jamison had one it. And he was thankful; it was easier to look at the face of the man now that his eyes weren't staring back.

BILLY YOU, NO MORE HILLS

"Mr. Cook, I'm real sorry you are no longer with us. and I want to thank you for all your help and friendship you gave me. I'm really and truly going to miss you." Then Billy looked up. "I don't know if Mr. Cook heard what I had to say. I know that he's up there with you now. So if you will tell him how I feel and how much I'm going to miss him, I will sure thank you."

Billy hesitated a moment then said, "Thank you."

Chapter 13

He didn't care or want to be around anyone for a while, so he went outside and ran up to the top of what he now called his hill. From up there up you could see the surrounding countryside and the neighborhood, with houses scattered here and there.

He heard the sound of a vehicle coming, and without looking, he knew it would be the hearse coming to take Mr. Cook's body away. He didn't want to witness this. He had already told the old cook goodbye. So now he moved over to the far corner of the fenced hill and sat and leaned back against a large oak tree that had probably been here longer than Mr. Cook had been on this earth.

He didn't know how long he had sat there, but he had probably dozed off for a while, when he heard someone coming up the hill. It was little Arthur.

Huffing and puffing, he came and sat down beside Billy.

After sitting for a while until he caught his breath, the young boy spoke. "Mrs. Jamison said that it was time for you to come down and have lunch."

At the bottom of the hill, he found a hamburger cookout going on.

The home had a big outdoor grill that was rarely used. It had to be a very special occasion before it was used.

Mrs. Jamison, the nurse, the teachers, and all the other help at the home were doing the cooking and preparation.

BILLY YOU, NO MORE HILLS

All the boys were laughing and joking as they stood in line waiting for their hamburger.

Mr. Cook was no longer with them, and it seemed the memory of him was already fading away. Except for Mrs. Jamison; Billy could tell by looking at her that she was a very sad lady, as she stood there turning hamburgers over.

Billy knew that Mrs. Jamison and the old cook had been real good friends.

The next day, the home had a new cook. She was a very, very large lady. She seemed to be always laughing and smiling. At each mealtime, she moved around through the mess hall, stopping to rest at each table, asking how the food was and, at the same time, teasing the boys and cutting up with them. She was an instant hit, and her meals were as good as the ones Mr. Cook had put out.

Now Billy no longer worked in the kitchen, and he was glad. He was back doing some of his old chores but not near as many.

Mrs. Jamison seemed to be taking it easy on him as of late. And when he ran into her or met her in some part of the building, she was much friendlier than she had been in the past.

He knew part of it was from going through the ordeal of finding Mr. Cook's dead body.

But he also knew that most of it was from his change in attitude. He had given up his cocky, swaggering ways and did what he was told without having a chip on his shoulder. The days slipped by, and winter was fast approaching. He still thought of Mr. Cook now and then, but his memory of the old cook seemed to be fading. But his memory of Elly was still very strong. Not a day went by that he didn't think of her, and he promised himself that never in the world would he ever forget her.

And Redheaded Mary slipped into his thoughts quite often. Maybe someday after he had become rich and famous, he would look her up and see if she still loved him.

She had kissed him, hadn't she? And you weren't supposed to kiss someone unless you loved them. That was his thinking on it.

Then one day, after things had settled down, after old Mr. Cook's passing and the boy's home had gotten back into its normal routine once more, Mrs. Jamison sent a message to Billy wanting to see him in her office. *What now?* he thought.

Her office door was open, and she said, "Come in, Billy." She folded her hands together and gave him a concerned and somewhat puzzled look.

"Billy, a very nice young couple have adopted Arthur, but he refuses to go with them and keeps on insisting that he see you."

"Why?"

"As if—why would anyone want to see you?" Billy thought that Mrs. Jamison didn't mean for it to sound that way, but it was, for sure, the way it came out. In the past he would have flared up at this, but now he forced himself to stay calm.

"Arthur is my little buddy. He comes to me when he has a problem." He stopped there; that would let her know the "why" part.

Mrs. Jamison went "Oh!" then added, "They are in the guest room. Would you please go in there and talk to Arthur and help them any way you can?"

Billy nodded his head. "Yes."

The guess room was a big, bright, pleasant room. This is where all the adopting parents come to visit with the kids they were expecting to adopt.

A nice-looking young couple, holding hands, were standing on one side of the room and little Arthur was on the opposite side, sitting on the floor with his back in a corner, his head hanging down, and not looking at his parents-to-be.

"Hey, buddy, what's wrong?"

The little boy let out a squeal and came running to Billy. "They are trying to take me away."

Dropping down on one knee, Billy put his arms around his young friend. "Well, what's wrong with that? You get to leave this old place and have a nice home with your own mother and father."

Arthur blurted out, "But I don't want to leave. All my friends are here, and you are my best friend of all." The little boy stepped back and, spreading his arms, added, "What would I do without you?"

BILLY YOU, NO MORE HILLS

Billy knew where his little buddy was coming from. Arthur had attached himself to Billy about the time he had begun to walk. Billy had been the one who picked him up when he fell down. The one that kissed his hurts away and the one that helped a boy that size with all his little needs.

A rush of sadness swept across Billy as it dawned on him what he was about to lose. Helping this young lad had meant as much to Billy as it had to Arthur.

A wave of sadness rushed over Billy; all the people he cared about were being taken away from him.

First it had been Redheaded Mary; he had to run off and leave her behind. Then came Elly—no way in the world could he ever get over losing her. Next, Mr. Cook—Billy had learned to like that rough old man; they had become friends. And now Arty, the little boy that had clung to Billy for love and protection. The young couple here would be able to give Arty more love and protection than he ever had. But in his heart he knew that it was going to be far better for Arthur to go and be part of his own family.

Billy put his arms around the little boy and hugged him tight then pushed him away, but keeping his hands on the little guy's shoulder, with faces inches apart. Keeping his voice low, he told Arty, "I'm not going to be here much longer either, buddy. You know when one of us turns eighteen, we have to leave the home, so it won't be long before I walk out that door and never come back."

He could see the little boy giving this a lot of thought, so he added, "You're lucky, you get to leave here right now with your own father and mother. You'll have your own bedroom, and I bet you will have your own TV and all kinds of toys to play with and a bunch of other nice things."

Now the lady was kneeling down beside them. "Arthur, you will have all that and much, much more, I promise you. Please come and live with us, please." Arthur turned to face her; she held her arms out.

"Would you let me hug you?" With a small hesitation, the little boy stepped into her arms, and the mother-to-be pulled him close in a tight hug. Then to Billy's absolute surprise, Arty put his arms around her neck and hugged her back.

Then of all things, the lady started crying. He couldn't understand grown-ups, especially grown-up women.

Well, his job was finished here. He knew what was happening was best for his little friend but didn't want to be here when they led him away, but as he reached the door to leave, the lady called out, "Billy."

He turned around, and there she was, with her arms around him, hugging him tight the same as she had her son-to-be. "Thank you, Billy, I thank you from the bottom of my heart." When she stepped back, there were still tears in her eyes. Then darned if she didn't lean forward and kiss him on the cheek.

Why were girls and women always hugging and kissing him? First it was Redheaded Mary, then Elly, and some of the ladies here at the home when Mr. Cook had passed away, and now this lady. *But*, Billy thought to himself, *why wouldn't it be him that was being kissed and hugged?* There was no doubt in his mind that he was the best-looking boy around here or anyplace else as far as he was concerned. But he wished they would stop it. He was just too old for this nonsense.

The days and weeks slipped by, and it was spring again. Billy had gotten back into the dull routine of the daily schedule here. He still went to the book room and studied each and every night. And every day that he could, he would run up this hill to stay in shape. Who knew, someday it might just save him again.

Then one day, as he was sitting in class with the other students, the large lady cook, without bothering to knock, came rushing into the room. Going straight to where the teacher was sitting behind her desk, she leaned over and whispered in her ear. All the kids were wondering what in the world was going on. Billy more so than the others, because both of the women were staring right at him.

The teacher stood up and clapped her hands. "OK. All of you, back to your books." Then looking back at Billy again, she wiggled her finger at him, saying, "Except for you. Please come up to my desk, Billy."

Needless to say, none of the other kids went back to their books; they were holding their breath, waiting to see what kind of trouble

BILLY YOU, NO MORE HILLS

Billy had gotten himself into now. Billy was wondering the same thing as he headed to the beckoning finger and went to where the teacher was sitting. The finger kept on wiggling until it pulled him down to where the teacher could whisper in his ear.

"Mrs. Jamison wants you in her office right now. Go."

As Billy went out the door, he was thinking, To be pulled out of the school room during a class, it had to be serious.

Behind him, he could hear the buzzing and the teacher clapping her hands again. "I said back to your studies—*now.*"

He headed for the office on dragging feet, wondering what he had done now. Trying to come up with it so he could have a good excuse as to why he did it. But nothing would come to mind. Sure, he had pushed Ralph into a corner and put his fist under his nose and threatened to punch him out if he didn't quit hulling the younger ones, but that was over a week ago. And he sure as heck would not be taken out of class for that.

He rapped lightly on the office door and took in a deep breath when told to come in. As Billy stepped into the room, he turned to run. He didn't believe in ghosts—well, not 100 percent anyway. But now he did because there was one standing in the middle of Mrs. Jamison's office. But before he could flee, the ghost held her arms out to him. Ghost or not, he went to Elly's open arms and hugged her back as hard as she hugged him.

Then he stepped back and said, "You're dead."

Elly whirled around a couple of times with her arms up in the air and answered, "Do I look dead?"

Boy she sure didn't, so Billy told her, "No, you don't, but your pants are still too tight." This brought a squeal of laughter from Elly, and she gave him another hug then did some more twirling around, saying, "Boy, if you have it, flaunt it."

This brought more laughter from the both of them, and to Billy's surprise, Mrs. Jamison joined in the laughing.

After this, there was a moment of silence, then stepping up close to Elly, Billy told her, "I went to the hospital and heard the doctor tell your parents that there was no hope and you were going to die."

She put her arms around him again and leaned her head against his, and in a soft voice said, "I did, Billy. I died twice—or so they tell me—but they brought me back to life both times. I don't know if I was just too tough to die or it just wasn't my time."

She took a deep breath and added, "But I was in the hospital a long, long time, I was in a deep coma, and the doctors didn't think that I would ever come out of it, but I showed them different, so here I am, and you're going to be stuck with me from now on. Boy, I've come to take you home."

Billy's eyes jumped wide as he looked at Mrs. Jamison to see what she had to say about this.

Elly placed her hand on his shoulder. "It's all right. Ester and I have been going over this for about a month now, getting the paperwork and all of the rest of it worked out." Then with her fist balled up, she slugged him on the shoulder, saying, "Boy, like it or not, you belong to me now."

He liked it, but who was this Ester person that Elly had mentioned? Then in awe, he knew. All the boys in the home had wondered what Mrs. Jamison's first name was, and some of them—well, most of them—had doubts that she even had a first name. Now Billy knew—Ester, Ester Jamison. He couldn't wait to get out of here and spread the word. But it didn't seem to be bothering her that he now knew her first name, and there was something else that puzzled Billy. Mrs. Jamison had been smiling when he entered her office and hadn't stopped smiling in all this time.

For all the years Billy had known her—and of course that was all his life—he had seen her smile two or three times at the most. Now look at her. It was Elly—it had to be Elly. She was so full of life and energy, so whenever she walked into a room, it lit the place up, and no matter if there was just one person in the room or a bunch, it seemed to brighten them up too.

Then Billy found out the real reason she was smiling so much. Elly became serious. "Billy, remember me telling you how much money I spent on the country club? Well, what a waste of money that was." She gave a big sigh. "Of course I was on a big ego trip, showing them all that I had more money than they did." She gave another big sigh. Then she grabbed him by the front of his shirt and pulled him to her, and in a very serious voice asked, "Do you think I'm all grown up, boy?"

"Nope!" he said because he didn't want her to. He hoped she would stay the same as she was forever.

Now Elly was pacing the floor. "Ester and I have been talking. Instead of me throwing my money away on places like the country club, I'm going to spend it right here." She spread her arms wide. "Right here on the Mayhill Boys' Home." Now she directed her words at Billy. "What do you think the boys need most, Billy?"

He didn't hesitate; he didn't have to take time to think about it. "A swimming pool, an indoor swimming pool."

She nodded. "They've got it." *Go for the works*, he thought.

"An indoor swimming pool it will be. What else?"

Billy glanced at Mrs. Jamison. Elly and she had already been talking about this, and that was the reason for the big smiles all over her face.

What else did the boys here need? Well, there were too many items to mention. So he had better shoot for the big and the best. "An indoor auditorium, with a basketball court and all." Another nod. "We'll start with those two, then later on go for more."

Once more, she was looking at Billy. "You know what, I think we'll name the auditorium after you. What do you want to call it?" He couldn't believe it; this he would have to think about. He didn't have a name, not a whole name—heck, they couldn't name an auditorium Billy, just plain old Billy. Then his face lit up in a big old smile. "Name it Billy You Auditorium."

This made both of the ladies laugh. Elly said, "I like it."

Mrs. Jamison nodded that she did too. So that meant Billy You would be the name of the auditorium when it was built.

Elly told them that she would get an architect and contractor to meet with Mrs. Jamison as soon as possible so that they could get started on both projects as soon as possible.

Then she added, "Now that all that is settled, when does this place feed around here? I'm starved." Billy started to speak up and say guests were only invited to eat with the boys on weekends and holidays, but Mrs. Jamison spoke up first.

"Oh my gosh, look at the time—they are starting to feed right now. Billy, take Elly to the mess hall and get her fed."

Well, Billy thought, *tell them you're going to spend a little money on the place and they sure treat you right.*

But this suited him fine. He was anxious to show Elly off to all the other kids in the home.

And as he led her into the mess hall, he got the results he expected and was hoping for. All activity stopped, and all eyes were riveted on the two of them as he led her toward his table.

Each and every boy was assigned a table, and that was where he sat to eat all his meals. There was no walking in and randomly sitting at any table you wanted to. The tables were oblong, and there was room for six kids at each table, and you sat in the same chair for all meals. There was a spare chair at the end of each table to be pulled out for visitors to sit in if you happened to have a visitor, which was very rare in this boys' home. But today, Billy had one, so he put on his best strut as he went to his table. He glanced over his shoulder to see how Elly was doing, and he couldn't believe what he saw. Her strut was putting his to shame. She was enjoying this more than he was. The other five boys were sitting as they approached the table, and now they all stood up as one, all eyes on Elly. The boy that would be sitting next to Elly on her left was a tall skinny boy with a long homely nose and a bobbing Adam's apple. He had a name, but all his friends called him Mortimer after a comic character they had seen on TV or the movies or someplace.

He went, "Wow, she's even prettier than you said, Billy."

Elly went around the corner of the table to him. "And what's your name?"

"Mortimer."

Elly put her arms around him and gave him a tight hug.

"That was a very nice compliment, Mortimer, thank you."

The next boy was a short chubby boy, always laughing and cutting up. He was friends with everyone. "You're even prettier than

BILLY YOU, NO MORE HILLS

Mortimer said you were," he told her. With a big smile on her face, Elly gave him his hug.

The other boys couldn't get words out fast enough to tell her how pretty she was, and all three of them got their hugs.

Now the whole mess hall was in an uproar. One of the older boys shouted, "You are the most beautiful lady in the whole world." Another one chimed in, "You're more beautiful the most beautiful lady in the whole wide world."And other comments and remarks along those lines came flowing from the rest of the boys. Billy could tell Elly was eating it up, enjoying every moment of it. Then to his surprise—well, not really to his surprise; he had learned to expect the unexpected from this woman. She had jumped upon the chair and then on the table and into one of her whirly dances with arms stretched high in the air. She was putting on quite a show, and the boys were going wild over it. They were jumping up and down, shouting, whistling, and clapping their hands, enjoying the show Elly was putting on.

Then she stopped it as fast as she had started it. She stopped her dancing, clapped her hands once, then held her arms up for quiet, and quiet she got. Then in a voice loud enough for all in the room to hear, she spoke up. "Boys, it's mealtime, and I've interrupted it long enough. Now we don't have time for me to go around and give you all a big hug today. But I promise you that Billy and I will come back to visit real often, and before it's over, I'll give each and every one of you a big hug."Billy thought there would be another outpouring of yelling and clapping, but there was none. And he knew why—so many of these boys had never been hugged in their entire lives. So they sat there in silent awe that a beautiful lady wanted to and was going to give them each a hug.

Needless to say, this was the most happy and fun-filled meal ever eaten in this room.

Then it was time to go.

Billy felt a rush of homesickness pass over him; this had been his home forever, and now he was leaving it. Leaving for good this time.

Out in front, Mrs. Jamison and Elly gave each other a good-bye hug.

Then Mrs. Jamison stepped over and put her arms around him. "Billy, I want you to go and have a wonderful life."

He put his arms around her, saying, "I've already had a wonderful life. From now on, it's going to get better."

As they were going down the steps, he looked back. Mrs. Jamison was standing there with her hands clasped together and tears in her eyes. Down through the years, Billy had misjudged the lady; she had been doing a job she had to do.

He was going to miss her.

As he turned, a big smile it lit up his face. He was going out to conquer the world like he had conquered these five steps he was walking down.

Yep, this boy they called Billy You was one lucky guy.

Now Mrs. Jamison was standing on the steps that Billy had just walked down. Two of the boys' home teachers were standing with her.

As the car carrying Billy away went out the gate and down the road, Mrs. Jamison pointed at it and said, "Through all the years I've been here and all the boys I've seen pass through here, if I could have adopted one of those boys, that boy going down the road there is the one I would have adopted."

The teachers standing there got a shocked look on their faces and spoke up. "Billy—you would have adopted Billy. Why, he's the one boy that gave us the most trouble." Mrs. Jamison's smile got wider, and with her hands still clasped together, she nodded her head yes.

"Yes, that boy going there is the one that gave us the most trouble."

Long after the car was out of sight, Mrs. Jamison was standing there looking down the road.

THE END

About the Author

Clarence Leslie is a World War II veteran, husband, and father of two. His entire life he has enjoyed telling stories to family and friend. He has carried many stories in his head over the years and at the age of 89, he would like to be able to share these stories from a lifetime of his experiences.

CPSIA information can be obtained
at www.ICGtesting.com
Printed in the USA
BVHW041929210623
666150BV00001B/141